Alex leaned forward in the darkness of the barn, telling himself not to be a fool. Then his hand touched hers. . . .

Emily felt herself shiver as a sensual lightning bolt jolted her. "I hope that's you."

"It is," he murmured. She was so close. He shouldn't be courting emotional danger like this, but he couldn't stop himself.

"You're not . . ." She paused, struggling to get the words out. "You're not going to kiss me or anything, are you?"

He leaned forward even more, until he could feel her breath on his face. "I don't think so."

"Good . . . Good . . . It wouldn't be a smart idea." She didn't pull away.

"Not smart," he agreed.

Then his mouth found hers in the smartest move he'd ever made. Her lips were warm, opening under his like a flower opening to the sun. He pressed her back into the hay, settling his body over hers, his mouth teasing and tormenting her until his blood was hotter than fire. He hungered for her, and her passionate response revealed just how much she wanted him. . . .

WHAT ARE *LOVESWEPT* ROMANCES?

They are stories of true romance and touching emotion. We believe those two very important ingredients are constants in our highly sensual and very believable stories in the *LOVESWEPT* line. Our goal is to give you, the reader, stories of consistently high quality that may sometimes make you laugh, sometimes make you cry, but are always fresh and creative and contain many delightful surprises within their pages.

Most romance fans read an enormous number of books. Those they truly love, they keep. Others may be traded with friends and soon forgotten. We hope that each *LOVESWEPT* romance will be a treasure—a "keeper." We will always try to publish

LOVE STORIES YOU'LL NEVER FORGET
BY AUTHORS YOU'LL ALWAYS REMEMBER

The Editors

Linda Cajio
The Reluctant Prince

BANTAM BOOKS
NEW YORK · TORONTO · LONDON · SYDNEY · AUCKLAND

THE RELUCTANT PRINCE
A Bantam Book / August 1992

If you would be interested in receiving protective vinyl
covers for your Loveswept books, please write to this address
for information:

Loveswept
Bantam Books
P.O. Box 985
Hicksville, NY 11802

ISBN 0-553-44273-2

Published simultaneously in the United States and Canada

For the one in my life who still believes in fairy tales and who still makes me believe. Thanks.

One

Emily Cooper stared at the submachine gun that stared right back at her.

"Peraco's a bargain this time of year," she muttered while slowly raising her hands in that worldwide gesture of "you've got the gun and I don't." "That's the last time I listen to my travel agent."

Nestled between Greece and Turkey, the Best Time Travel agent had told her the tiny country of Peraco had lots of sun, lots of sky blue Aegean sea, lots of rich casino players, lots of cheap rates, and a coronation about to happen.

Wanna bet? Emily thought, swallowing back a lump of cold fear. The head of Peraco's army, General Florian Kiros, had been unhappy with his elder sister's inheriting the crown. Two days before the coronation, he had cut off the borders and the sea in a coup so swift, everyone was still scrambling to figure out how it had happened. Now people were rioting, either for or against the general, and the capital city of Seriat was in chaos.

In the moonlight, Emily could see that the male facing her was young, barely an adult, and that made her situation even more dangerous. Young men panicked faster than older ones. Especially when foolish tourists blundered into them as she had. What a way to soothe a failed marriage and broken engagement. Next time she'd read a good book.

The young man called out softly into the dark alley behind him. Clearly, there were others with him. Just what she needed. A party.

"I'm an American," she whispered to him, hoping he understood English.

He shoved the gun out toward her in an unmistakable gesture.

"Okay, I'm not an American," she said, raising her hands even higher.

"You sound like one," came a deep whisper from the edge of the alley. It was followed by a man, a real one this time. As he stepped into the moonlight, she noted he was tall, dark, and in his thirties. Close enough to middle age, she thought happily. Like the young man, he wasn't wearing a uniform, just blue jeans and a jacket. Several other men joined him. She could feel waves of suspicion emanating from the group. She wasn't out of the woods yet.

The tall one's voice sounded straight out of a good old American Ivy League school, though. In fact, if she weren't so scared, she would appreciate him more.

"Thank goodness," she said, although she didn't lower her hands. "I'm trying to get to the American Embassy and I'm lost."

"Stanni?" the man asked the one with the gun, completely ignoring her.

"She was just standing here." He tilted the barrel slightly upward, but not enough for Emily to relax.

"Please," one of the other men begged. "We must go, Highness."

Everyone hissed at the man who'd spoken. The poor soul looked mortified and immediately corrected himself.

"Ah . . . Alex."

It was too late. Emily stared at the tall, dark man in wonder. Highness? He was a *Highness*?

"What are you a Highness of?" she asked, her irrepressible curiosity rising to the surface. "Are you a prince? Are you a *king*? Where did you get that accent? Harvard?"

The other men burst into chatter she couldn't understand. They all waved and pointed at her as if she'd grown two heads. Emily had a feeling she'd asked the wrong questions.

"Why aren't you safe and sound at a hotel?" the Highness man named Alex finally asked her. He looked thunderous at the giveaway.

"Because I wasn't about to be rounded up and hauled off to Lord knows where," she snapped. "Hey, you can be the Highness of East Jipip and I promise not to tell a soul." She nodded to the one called Stanni. "Can he put the gun down now?"

"They've rounded up tourists?" Alex asked, ignoring her request.

She nodded again. "At the Colonnade they have. I managed to escape down the back stairs with several others, but then we got separated trying to get to the embassy. If you boys could just point the way—"

"Florian must be insane to be rounding up

tourists," he said to the others, who looked grim and nodded.

He was on first-name terms with the perpetrator of this fiasco? Emily thought. She decided getting out of there was her major priority and waved her raised hands. "Now that you know I'm a nice, normal American . . . can I put these down so you can show me the way to the embassy?"

The man didn't answer. Instead, he said in a cold voice, "This isn't a stroll in the park. How did you get this far avoiding trouble?"

"I don't know," she said. She had the distinct feeling she was on trial. "I hid whenever I heard something . . . which was about every three seconds."

Her little band of tourists had walked away from the hotel and right into a major riot. Everyone had scattered, and she in the wrong direction. She had wandered the back streets, hoping to come across the embassy by herself. That she had avoided trouble so far was a miracle.

"Look," she began, eyeing the gun. Her fear level had dissipated to general wariness. "I'm just a kindergarten teacher from Warminster, Pennsylvania, who's tired and scared and lost. All I want to do is put my hands down and go the embassy, okay?"

"Where is the Statue of Liberty?" one of the others asked in heavily accented English.

"New York City," she said obediently. Her arms were getting tired, so she'd go along with anything to be done with these men.

"Who lives in Hollywood?" asked another.

"Ah . . ." She wondered desperately *who* was the who he was thinking of. "Movie stars?"

"Clint Eastwood," the man said triumphantly.

"Actually, he lives in Carmel," she corrected him.

The man frowned darkly. "Hollywood!"

"Hollywood," she hastily agreed.

"Who won World Series?" the first asked.

"How the hell do I know?" she said between clenched teeth. The man muttered dubiously.

"There's an easy way to verify her story," Alex said. "Let's see your passport."

"I . . ." Emily swallowed. She had a feeling he wasn't going to like this. "I lost it with my purse. I only have my one bag."

She turned the forefinger of one upraised hand down and pointed to the flight bag at her feet.

"You don't have your passport?" He looked ominous. "How could you not have your passport?"

"Well, I—"

"High—Alex, please. We *must* go now!" her questioner on things American urged. "Leave the woman and let's go."

"Cosmo's right," young Stanni said. "We must go . . . but we must take the woman with us. She knows too much."

Emily gaped at him. "I don't know anything, and I'm not going *anywhere* with *anybody*!"

Noise erupted at the other end of the street. People were running around the corner, shouting and smashing windows in a shower of glass. Soldier-filled Jeeps squealed into view to quell the rioters.

"Duck!" Alex yelled, then grabbed her arm and pulled her down the alley with the rest of the men. She stumbled over her flight bag and snatched it up, not daring to lose the last piece of herself in this vacation hell.

They ran, all of them, their feet clattering on the cobblestones. The noise sounded louder than a submachine gun to Emily's terrified senses. When they reached a high wooden fence, the men boosted themselves over it. Alex put his hand under her backside and hoisted her into the air. Emily squawked in surprise and indignation, then seized the squared planks and threw herself over to the other side.

She fell to the ground, just missing some trash cans. Out of the corner of her eye, she saw Alex vault effortlessly over the fence. Wonderful, she thought. She was with a Schwarzenegger devotee.

"Let's go!" He yanked her to her feet, whether she was ready or not.

She wasn't. She stumbled along, and the only thing keeping her upright was his hand like iron on her arm.

They crept around corners and down alleyways, always keeping to the shadows, until she was dizzy with confusion. Not that she knew where she was anyway.

Stanni called something to Alex in their native language. He answered back sharply. All Emily knew in Peracan was how to ask where the library and bathroom were, but she didn't need a translator to know their conversation was about her.

She was gasping for breath, gulping it into her lungs in a desperate attempt to get oxygen to her screaming muscles. She couldn't run much farther, and if she couldn't run much farther . . .

Alex yanked her into a doorway.

"Patrol," he whispered. She heard the whine of a Jeep as he dragged her through the door and into a dark hallway.

As the Jeep passed without stopping, she realized they were in the lobby of an apartment building. She also realized that Alex had her plastered to the wall, his body pressed protectively over her. Every inch of his torso was against hers, breast to chest, hip to hip, thigh to thigh. He was leaner than she'd thought. He was holding her arms to her sides, and her nose was buried in his shoulder. The man-scent of him filled her senses.

"At least you didn't scream," he said, his mouth at her ear.

She lifted her chin, trying to inhale ordinary air rather than disturbingly virile man. "Why would I scream?"

"To bring them in on us."

Her blood boiled instantly, and she pushed against him. "Dammit, I am not some spy! Do I sound like James Bond? Look like James Bond?"

He grinned. "Actually you look more like Octopussy—"

She stamped on his foot.

"Ouch!" He immediately let her go. "What did you do that for?"

She smiled. "Satisfaction."

The door was pushed open. They froze. A man was silhouetted on the threshold.

"Alex?" The whisper was Stanni's. He stepped inside. "Alex?"

"Here," Alex said softly.

Other bodies crowded in the doorway as the rest of the men came in. They moved around Alex protectively. She still didn't know who he was, but obviously these men considered him valuable, and judging from his earlier comment, he opposed General Kiros's coup. Not the kind of guy she wanted to get caught with, no matter how good-looking he was.

"Well, boys, it's been fun," she said, smiling brightly. "Now I'll just mosey along to the embassy—"

"I wish you could," Alex said. "But I'm afraid you'll have to stay with us. Clearly the streets aren't safe for you—"

"Oh no I won't," she said, backing away from him.

He snorted in exasperation. "Believe me, I don't want to be stuck with you, but there's no choice. You have to come with us."

"I don't know who you are and I don't care." No imposing presence would keep her from her appointed quest. "I need to go to the embassy."

"You can't."

Emily had had enough of this. She was an American and she knew her rights. "I'm an American and I know my rights. The hell I can't go."

"That's right, you can't," Alex snapped. "For one thing, you'd have to be an idiot not to know I'm not your average American male. I can't have you wandering around with that information. But more important, half the city's erupting in riots. It simply isn't safe for you to be wandering alone. Now I've said you can't go on by yourself tonight, and you can't."

She stared at him, her mouth open and her brain numb. He had delivered his speech with all the authority of the lord of the manor. Certainly, the other men thought he was, because they now crowded around her, effectively cutting off any escape.

"Let's all shut up and move," Alex said.

They all shut up and moved—Emily Cooper, lost tourist, included.

. . .

Alex Kiros knocked four times before the door opened a crack. It was enough.

"Quickly!" Tuno said, reaching out and pulling Alex inside. The others scrambled in behind him, and the door closed against the night.

The old man wrapped him in a hug, dampening Alex's shoulder with his tears. He hugged him back, grateful the elderly retainer was still safe and well despite the chaos.

"My aunt?" he asked in Peracan.

"Her Royal Highness got out safely," Tuno said.

Alex sighed with relief. He hadn't been to the palace in two days, not able to get anywhere near it. He couldn't believe he and the men from his office had made it this far.

"What a mess," Tuno went on. "The city's in chaos, the utilities are out, and your uncle is running rampant. I don't think it could get worse, but it probably will."

Alex glanced around the room lit only by candles. He hadn't realized utilities had been cut. The news was ominous.

"Who is this?" Tuno asked, peering at their most recent companion. The woman was standing with her back against the front door, as if trying to press herself straight through the wood to the outside.

"An American tourist we stumbled over," Alex said, turning to look at her.

The candles on the table by the door illuminated her features. Her skin was slightly reddened, as if she had been cramming in overtime on Peraco's beaches. Her gray eyes were wide and wary, giving her a hunted look.

Her shoulder-length brown hair was tied back in a makeshift ponytail, strands falling out and around her face. She was tall and slim, dressed in jeans and a lightweight navy sweater that draped nicely over her firm breasts. Not beautiful, Alex thought, but somehow memorable. She definitely had the look of a small-town all-American girl. He hadn't lived in the States for more than fifteen years without knowing that image.

She also looked scared to death. He supposed he couldn't blame her, but the last thing he needed was to be stuck with a lost tourist. If only Cosmo hadn't blurted out the wrong thing . . .

"She has my hospitality, of course," Tuno said, drawing his attention. The older man bowed graciously to her and held out his hand. "My name is Tuno," he said in English. "I'm afraid the amenities are not as I would like to offer, but I do have some food and a roof."

The woman smiled tremulously and took his hand. "You give me a feast and a palace."

Tuno laughed. "There was a time when I could have. But you honor an old widower with your graciousness."

Tuno led her to the bedroom, off to the left. Alex watched her, fighting the urges to let her go as she'd requested and to protect her from the political storm raging through Seriat.

The men who'd accompanied him shuffled their feet restlessly. "We must go to our families now," Cosmo said.

Alex nodded, knowing they were worried. He shook their hands and thanked them, for they'd risked much to see him there unscathed.

Stanni stripped off the gun he'd found and handed it to Alex, who grinned. It looked more dangerous than it was, having no bullets. The young man had been sent by his aunt Julia to warn him that his uncle Florian was rounding up family members, even ones as low and obscure as he, for a "public show of support" at his coronation. Stanni had been cool, collected, and invaluable ever since. Alex clapped him in a rough embrace.

"I'll be back when I have news," Stanni promised.

"You better," Alex said. People were rioting in support of Julia, the named heir to the throne, and clashing with those who supported Florian, the eldest male. Alex just wanted to get the hell out.

He shook his head. What a time to come home and open a branch of his computer business. He wished he'd paid more attention to the rumblings after his grandfather, the Crown Prince, had died a little over a month ago, but he'd never thought Florian would be this insane. Who would?

Florian's father, Alex's grandfather, had collected broken clocks, not to fix them, but just to have them. Alex's own father had a horror of work in any form, and literally broke out in hives whenever he had to discuss his investments with his banker. Even the named heir, Julia, Florian's sister, preferred sleeping with her Irish wolfhounds—innocently, of course—rather than her husband. Alex's various cousins all had quirks, ranging from breeding snakes to sculpting in pig iron. He himself worked hard at living a normal, everyday life. It still amazed him that his family thought he was the nut.

Alex closed and locked the door after the last man left. His stomach growled, reminding him that food had been a hit-or-miss affair lately. He remembered his new companion had been on the run too. She might want something to eat, and maybe a little hospitality on his part would help negate what had happened earlier.

In the kitchen he set some cheese and fruit on a tray, along with a bottle of wine. He didn't want to take too much from Tuno, knowing food supplies would become a problem if the coup continued.

When he walked into the bedroom, Tuno was alone.

"What the hell! Where is she?" Alex dumped the tray on the bed and stalked toward the curtained window. "Why didn't you call? She knows who I am—"

"She's in the bathroom," Tuno said. "Calm down, boy."

"Who knows what calm is anymore?" Alex muttered.

"You obviously don't. Keep your head." Tuno gave him a stern look. "I've been talking to her, and she says you kidnapped her."

"Well," Alex began, running his fingers through his hair and wondering how to explain this to the former palace majordomo. Tuno had never let him get away with anything when he was young. "In a way, I suppose I have. There was a riot in the street and we ran . . . and took her with us."

"Because she knows who you are and you don't want your uncle to find you," Tuno finished.

"Well-l-l-l. It is that. But she doesn't know exactly who I am. However, it isn't safe for anyone out there, especially a lone woman tourist. I'll take her to the embassy in the morning, when it's safer." Alex's mouth tightened and he said bluntly, "I'm staying out of this, Tuno. I only came here to start a branch of my computer company. The family can indulge their excesses and squabble among themselves. They've been doing it for years. I've always hated all the intrigues, you know that. All I want to do is get out and go home to the States."

Tuno frowned. "Naming his heir is about the only right left to our Crown Prince. Your grandfather took advantage of that to break with the tradition of naming the eldest son, and named Julia, his eldest child, his successor instead. A smart thing, I say. Florian was always wild, too wild. Once I caught him kicking a sentry at the main gate, trying to break the man's concentration. And that was when he was only three! Now look at what he's done. It's outraged the world, Alex."

"I just want to go back to the States, Tuno. Where *I* belong," Alex said stubbornly. "I've made my life there since college."

"Then why haven't you just presented yourself to Florian?" Tuno asked. "What do you care who is crowned? All you have to do is pose for the required picture of support and your uncle will let you go home. He'd be happy to see the back of you."

The bathroom door opened before he could answer Tuno.

"Thank you, Tuno," the woman said as she stepped into the bedroom. "There's something wonderfully romantic about using the facilities by candlelight."

Tuno laughed. "Next time I woo a woman, I'll have to remember that."

Alex noticed that she'd brushed her hair into a better ponytail, and she looked as if she'd washed her face. A face that was more striking than his first glance had shown, although her eyes glistened as if she'd been crying. He became aware of his own lack of basic soap and water. But he'd been stuck in his office for two days altering and hiding government records his company had in data bases. When had he had time for amenities?

"See what my Alexi has brought for you," Tuno said, pointing to the tray. Half the contents had slid off it and onto the bed when Alex had dumped it.

She practically pounced on the food. She picked up an apple and a pear, biting into one and then the other.

"Lord, but that's good," she mumbled with her mouth full.

"Why didn't you put out some meat?" Tuno asked, frowning at Alex.

"You didn't have much," Alex said as he picked up a second apple to eat. "You need to save it for yourself, Tuno. Food could get scarce if this continues for much longer."

"Bah. The meat will go bad in another day without refrigeration," Tuno said. "Don't worry. Something will turn up."

"Just don't carry the Mr. Micawber imitation too far," Alex warned.

"This is wonderful. Really," the woman said. "Especially after only crackers from my hotel room and the stale cookies that were still in my flight bag."

"How appalling. I insist you eat properly." Tuno strode out of the room.

Alone with the woman, Alex decided to get questions answered. "What's your name?"

She stiffened, her wariness returning instantly.

"I'm not going to hurt you," he said, exasperated. "I'm not an ogre. I'm just like you. I only want to go home." He realized he'd make more progress by being freer with her. "I'm Alex Kiros."

She raised her eyebrows, then said, "Emily Cooper."

"Emily Cooper," he repeated, trying it on his tongue. It was so all-American, he'd bet her father was a fullback. "Why did you pick Peraco for a vacation?"

"Because I listened to an idiotic travel agent," she replied, looking at the fruit in her hands. She set them aside. "Because I had a tight budget and I wanted a complete getaway, even down to the miles. Peraco seemed like the perfect place." She laughed wryly. "It looks like it even has its own adventure game."

That odd urge to protect her ran through him again. As he stared at her, the air became charged with a tension that seemed to drag him toward her, even though neither of them moved. As his gaze swept over her of its own volition, he grew increasingly aware that they were alone in the room. She was so remote from what was happening, like an oasis of home in a desert. She reminded him of healing sunshine, cool lemonade, easy talk, and intimate smiles.

He reached out and touched her cheek, and was instantly enraptured by the softness of her skin. Her eyes widened, then she turned her face away. He pulled back his hand, shocked by that irresistible urge to touch her.

What was it about her that provoked this kind of reaction in him? Especially one so strong. It made no sense. But then nothing made any sense anymore.

He set his half-eaten apple down, forcing aside the sensual interest she aroused in him. "The world won't stand for this," he said.

"The world didn't stand for Hitler either, but it took years to get rid of him."

The thought was sobering.

"Are you really a member of the royal family?" she asked. Curiosity shone in her eyes.

He shrugged. She'd learned enough already, so the rest wouldn't hurt. "A very low one. I'm the youngest son of the youngest son."

"You sound like Sinbad. Do you have a title?"

"I'm a prince, actually. But I don't use it. It makes me sound like a police dog. Just Alex will do."

She shook her head. "I thought you were an American."

"I have dual citizenship. I've been in the States since I went to Princeton."

"That's appropriate."

He chuckled, liking her quick wit. "I suppose."

"So why all the rigamarole? Clearly, you don't inherit the crown, so why this secrecy? Why kidnap me the way you did?"

"I didn't kidnap you," he corrected her. "It wasn't safe for you, so I merely carried you along."

"Could have fooled me," she muttered, just loud enough for him to hear.

"Look, if my uncle gets a hold of me, he'll use me in some way. I can't afford for him to discover where I am."

"I promise I won't tell him. Why can't you believe me?"

He said nothing.

They were silent for a moment, then she said in

a small voice, "Tuno says there's rioting everywhere in the city."

He nodded. "I'm the better choice at the moment, Emily Cooper. Honest."

"No," she said, her tone rising sharply. "I won't stay here. I have to go now. My parents will be so worried, my brothers . . . my students. Kindergartners don't handle disappearing teachers well."

"You have to stay tonight," he said firmly, determined to convince her. It was for her own safety, of course. But Alex was honest enough to admit that he didn't want to lose the chance to spend even just one evening with this woman.

"What about your family back in the States?" she asked. Don't you want to get back to them?"

"I don't have any." One ex-wife didn't count. "My family's here."

"Oh." She nodded. "Tuno."

"Tuno's an old friend. My parents are in Paris right now, for which I am eternally grateful."

"Well, I can't impose on your friends," she said, picking up her flight bag.

"Don't be an idiot." He moved to block her way to the door. "You can't go out there tonight. I'll take you to the embassy in the morning."

"I'm not staying with a bunch of strangers!" She waved a hand, and he could feel her desperation building. "I won't take food from those who need it or endanger them because of my presence. If I have to turn myself in, then I will. But I'm going."

She had guts and integrity, he thought. A little too much of both for her own good, however. "I will not allow you to go."

She eyed him for one long moment. "I'm going."

He didn't need this. He told himself he just

ought to let her go, since she was so insistent. But he knew he couldn't.

Crossing his arms over his chest and spreading his legs, he assumed a deliberately masculine pose, emphasizing their difference in size.

"You'll go when I say you'll go and not before," he said, and smiled grimly. "So between now and tomorrow morning, I'll be your Siamese twin."

He sat down on the bed and picked up his apple. "Make yourself comfortable."

She looked from him to the door, then back at him. Sighing, she gave up and plunked down beside him.

Two

The lazy gray light of dawn was just filtering through the windows as Emily and Alex prepared to leave Tuno's apartment. Tuno hugged Alex and then Emily, to her surprise. His grip was fierce.

"Thank you for everything," she whispered. Tears caught at the back of her throat. It was lack of sleep, she thought, trying to explain away the sudden flood of emotions. She appreciated the old man's kindness more than she could express. Oddly enough, she trusted Tuno. Despite Alex's macho display the night before, Tuno was the reason she'd decided it would be best to stay until morning. Unfortunately, once she found out what Alex meant by being Siamese twins, she'd wished she'd left.

He'd slept in the same room with her, on the floor. She hadn't slept. How could she with a handsome hunk of a prince five feet away?

Imagine, little ordinary Emily Cooper had spent the night with a prince. And imagine if they'd spent the night together the way her fantasies had urged. She didn't need *that.* This whole thing was unreal enough, without the complication of suffering a physical twinge of arousal over a man. Okay, so it was more like a convulsion, but she wasn't about to be more stupid than she'd already been on this Vacation from Hell. The only thing that kept her from complete panic was the knowledge that she was on her way back home. Rowdy, wonderful kids, endless arguments over curriculum, meetings with parents in the Teachers' Room, and the occasional date with Mr. Lifeless was reality.

"I don't like this," Tuno muttered.

"Don't like what?" Alex asked.

Emily now caught a trace of an accent in that deep voice of his, almost indiscernible to the average ear. Hers seemed to be unaverage lately. And that faint accent, Lord help her, was unbearably sexy.

"You and Emily going out there alone," Tuno replied.

He'd argued strongly that he should be the one to take her to the embassy rather than Alex, and after losing that argument, he'd started a new one that she and Alex should stay for safety's sake. She couldn't stay. Staying frightened her on so many levels. The whole damnable situation did. And the tall man by the door scared her almost more than anything else.

Tuno went on. "Your aunt cannot afford to have you caught, Alexi."

"I doubt I'm worth anything to Florian. But don't worry." Alex smiled. "This will just be a simple walk to the embassy and back. I won't be gone more than a couple of hours. You'll see."

He opened the door, peered out, then motioned for her.

Emily swallowed back a sudden lump of uneasiness. Fatigue was like wool around the edges of her brain, hampering her thinking process. She didn't want to go out there. Deep down she finally admitted she was grateful she'd been kidnapped and given this safe haven.

"Miss Cooper," Alex prompted.

"Okay, okay." She took a deep breath and followed him outside.

All her fears instantly rushed to the surface. The street was completely deserted, and not a light showed from any of the windows of the other homes. It was unnatural . . . surreal, like a Salvatore Dali landscape. Emily shivered.

"Quick," Alex murmured, urging her forward.

They moved quietly along the street, single file. Emily focused her gaze on Alex's back. It was a long back, tapering from wide shoulders to trim hips. The muscles were obvious, even through his shirt. His brown hair brushed his collar, the expensive cut holding its shape without benefit of a blow-dryer. His hair looked silky, too, and she wondered how it would feel. Her hands had actually lifted to touch him, when she realized what she was doing, and snatched her hand back. What the hell was the matter with her? Men who needed help were trouble. She'd learned that lesson long ago. She thought she'd broken her automatic response to try to solve helpless men's problems. But these were extraordinary circumstances, and being kidnapped by a prince topped them all. She wondered if this was how the Stockholm Syndrome began, when a kidnap victim became sympathetic to, even enamored of, the kindly kidnapper.

"Naaah," she muttered to herself. She couldn't be *that* stupid.

As they turned corners and crept down more deserted, unnaturally quiet streets, the silence grew foreboding. Absolutely no one was moving in this part of Seriat. Emily realized she hadn't even heard a car motor. The only noise was their shoes slapping quietly on the concrete. Wisps of mist not yet burnt off by the rising sun floated along the air like slow-moving ghosts. The chill dawn sea breeze found its way under her sweater and jeans. Goosebumps rose on her skin, and she shivered, half from the breeze and half from dread. Her stomach flipped over sickeningly. A compulsion rose in her to make some kind of noise to dispel the growing tenseness. She had an awful feeling that if she didn't, she'd wind up screaming in a sudden burst of terror. Alex probably wouldn't like that.

"Looks like everybody's sleeping off the riot," she said. Her voice sounded hollow.

"Let's hope so." He snorted. "What a damn mess."

"It could be worse."

He glanced back at her, his expression skeptical. "How?"

"Good question," she mumbled, realizing her inane attempt at conversation was more inane than she'd thought. "Maybe you better not be doing this. Tuno's pretty worried about you."

"He seems to think I'm worth more than I am." He shrugged. "I've always been the, I don't know, ugly duckling of the family."

Emily quickened her pace to walk beside him and stared at him in disbelief. His eyes were dark brown, almost black. It was hard to read the expression in them, but it seemed to be wistful. His nose was straight, his cheekbones pronounced, his jaw firm. His mouth was sensual, with a slight droop to the lower lip that promised passion. Combined with a lean body, the last thing he looked like was an ugly duckling.

"You've got to be kidding," she said.

He shrugged again in that completely European way that meant "That's your privilege," and she wondered whether to believe him. Whatever, he'd certainly become a humdinger of a swan.

He glanced over at her. "You said you were a kindergarten teacher."

"Somebody's got to do it." But she smiled.

"You really like your students, don't you?"

She nodded. "Five-year-olds are always unpredictable. Each year I think no group could surprise me more, and each year they do."

"I would think so." He chuckled, then sobered. "I'm sorry I had to bring you along. But you understand that it was for your safety."

"And yours," she reminded him.

"No. Not really." He looked forward, away from her. "The city is very dangerous right now. You couldn't be out here alone. I wouldn't have been able to live with myself if I hadn't tried to help you."

Chivalry is not dead, Emily thought, then groaned silently. She'd have that Stockholm Syndrome for sure if she kept this up. "Well, it's done now. I suppose it doesn't matter as long as I get to the embassy."

"I'll get you there, I—"

The sudden squealing of tires interrupted him. They froze, listening as a motor was gunned to zooming speed, then a Jeep rounded the corner, heading straight toward them.

"Run!" Alex shouted. He grabbed her hand and dragged her behind him as he dashed toward an alleyway.

She nearly beat him as they raced around the corner building. She would have kept on running, but he yanked her back against the wall. She flattened herself to it automatically.

"What the hell are you doing?" she whispered, when he peeked around the edge of the building. Her breath whistled loudly in and out of her lungs. She swallowed in air, trying to regain control of her bursting heart.

"I'm checking," he said. "They didn't stop, whoever they are. Listen, can't you hear the Jeep in the distance?"

"I can't hear anything except my lungs sounding like a beached whale's. Are you sure they've gone?"

"Sure." He looked around the alley they were in. It was narrow, barely wide enough for a car, and it had more than its fair share of uncollected trash. "I think it's safe to go out—"

"Let me know when you *know*," she said. "I'm damned if I'm going out there again because you 'think' it's safe. I bet they told that to Custer before they sent him off to the Little Bighorn."

"We can't hide here," he said, scowling down at her.

"Sure we can. Just lean back and relax."

"I've got to get you to the embassy. That's where *you* want to go, remember?"

She smiled sweetly. "I can wait."

He muttered under his breath. Emily couldn't quite make it out, but she had a feeling her ancestors weren't coming out on the good end of the stick. She didn't care. She wanted to get to the embassy, she wanted to get there in one piece, and she didn't intend to go out there again until she had that guarantee. In writing.

"We could go down the alleyways," he said.

"Thanks, but no thanks."

She could actually see him clamping his jaw together. She might be obtuse, but every bone in her body, every primal instinct she possessed, was screaming at her not to go out there again. They were a couple of rank amateurs who should be surrounded by James Bond, the Saint, the Avengers, Secret Agent, and the A-Team, with Mr. T. leading the pack. She understood that now.

"We'll create more attention if we continue to stand here," he said finally. "Everyone in these buildings can see us, you know."

"They can?" She glanced upward. Window upon window stared down at her. She groaned inwardly, feeling trapped. "Okay, okay."

"Don't worry," he said. "We'll get you to the embassy."

"Somebody better," she muttered. Otherwise, she couldn't make any promises about her actions.

They took more turns, and more turns, running between the buildings. Crossing the street to the next alleyway was sheer terror. The alley held a sameness that was comforting at first, but then became more troubling as a feeling of isolation stole over her. She couldn't see street signs or what the homes were like to give her an idea of where they were. She remembered passing the embassy coming in from the airport, but it seemed to her the area had been less residential. She felt

completely disoriented and could only trot behind
Alex, trusting him. After all, he grew up here.

Still, as they twisted and turned down more
alleys, and as the sun grew higher and brighter in
the sky, Emily got a funny feeling in the pit of her
stomach.

"Do you know where we are?" she asked.

"Well, not too far," he replied, frowning.

"You *don't* know where we are, do you?"

"We're in Seriat."

"Alex, you lived here for years!"

"Shhh!" he hissed at her. "You're the one who
insisted on staying in the damn alleyways. And I
haven't lived here for years too. Nearly twenty of
them. I can't tell anything from back here, and
there aren't any street signs."

"I'm not with James Bond," she said. "I'm with
Harry Crumb."

"If I could see some street signs, Ms. Cooper," he
gritted out between clenched teeth, "we would be
at the embassy now."

"All right already. I get the point." She turned,
ready to march out to the nearest street sign and
get them on their way.

He yanked her back. "Cautiously, please. I may
not be James Bond, but I have that much sense."

She glanced heavenward for salvation. It'd be a
miracle if she got it down here.

The streets were better this time. There were no
more surprises in the form of careening cars, and
no patrols. That was rather odd, but Emily wasn't
about to question that gift. If the usurper thought
he'd secured the city well enough to dismiss patrols, she wouldn't complain.

Things began to look more commercial. Shops
and touristy cafes outnumbered the homes, and

there were even a few people on the streets. They didn't look at her and Alex as they scurried by, and she and Alex didn't look at them.

"The embassy isn't much farther," he said, grinning down at her.

"Pleased with yourself, aren't you?" she asked dryly.

"I think I'm allowed."

"After the alley fiasco?"

"You are picky, do you know that?"

"It's the kidnappee's right."

"I guess I didn't look at the rule book."

"I'll say."

The playfulness was the only outward sign of the anticipation she was feeling. And she could feel it in Alex too. This had all been an incredible adventure, but it was just about over. She was almost on her way home.

As euphoria rose in her, noise filtered to them. Alex looked at her and raised his eyebrows. "The embassy's on the next street. Does it sound like a traffic jam to you?"

She shrugged. "It's probably everyone trying to get into the embassy."

But it wasn't. They flattened themselves in a doorway when a military Jeep shot by on the nearest cross street. Emily's heart thumped heavily in her chest. A one-ton vise was squeezing her lungs again.

"Alex."

"It's okay."

Somehow their hands found each other, and the fear receded slightly when his strong fingers closed around hers. She felt like an icicle against the warmth radiating from him. It raised her body temperature even as it lowered her apprehension.

But her apprehension took a jump forward again when she realized the noise hadn't abated with the passing Jeep.

"Maybe I better go and see," Alex said.

She tightened her hand around his in a death grip. "Oh no. You're not leaving me here by myself."

They crept out of the doorway together and cautiously made their way to the cross street. Emily peeked around Alex as he peeked around the corner. Her heart plummeted a thousand feet at the sight that greeted them.

Jeeps and soldiers sporting the Peracan emblem swarmed everywhere in front of the United States Embassy. A tank had taken up position to one side. Beyond the embassy fence, she could see marine guards at attention behind several men in business suits who were arguing loudly with two officers. A group of people, civilians by their clothes, were standing to the side. The atmosphere was tense in what was an obvious show of force on General Florian's part. But the most telling feature of all was the high wrought-iron gates to the embassy compound closed against everything.

Even if she were able to run the gauntlet, she couldn't get in. And the people inside couldn't get out.

Emily gasped, then gasped again as tears began to flow down her cheeks. She couldn't believe what she was seeing. It was impossible.

Alex cursed and ducked them back into the doorway again. "That explains why we didn't run into patrols earlier," he said. "They're all at the embassies." He turned to look at her and caught the tears. Smiling gently, he wiped them away. "It'll be okay, Emily."

"Why?" she asked, sniffling and swiping at her suddenly running nose.

He reached in his pocket and pulled out a handkerchief, handing it to her. "I don't know."

She dabbed at fresh tears. This had to be a dream. She'd never get home. Never. Then she realized she was giving up without a fight.

"I'm going," she said, straightening and squaring her shoulders. "I'm an American citizen. They can't stop me from entering my own embassy. It's against all the international laws."

He gaped at her, then shook his head. "No you're not."

"You can't stop me." She had to go. Had to. Had to!

"The hell I can't. I'm responsible for you—"

"Since when?" she snapped.

"Since I found you wandering the streets by yourself last night."

"Don't be a hypocrite, Alex. You kept me because you were afraid I'd give you away."

His glare was thunderous. "You've got a long way to go if you think that."

She glared back at him.

He took a deep breath, clearly to control his temper, and checked their surroundings. "Emily, be sensible. You won't make it through and you know it. Didn't you see those people? I think they're being held from going in. If Florian has gone this far, there's no telling what he'll do with them. It's not safe here. Not now."

"I'm going."

"You're not going."

"I'm going, and you can't stop me!" Her voice was becoming dangerously loud.

He immediately covered her mouth with his hand. "Emily, use your brain! You can't go to the embassy. It's impossible. We'll go back to Tuno's and wait a little while longer. Come up with something else. I know there's some common sense in there. All you've got to do is find it, woman!"

His words penetrated her numbness. She knew he was right, and she hated him for it. Her cheeks felt oddly wet. She realized she was crying again and slumped against him. He took his hand away from her mouth and wrapped his arms around her in comfort.

"How am I supposed to get home?" she whispered, clutching his shirt.

"We'll get you home. Trust me, please. Somehow, I'll get you home."

They stood there together, unmindful for the moment of the danger. Emily's panic attack faded. She felt alone . . . and not alone. Alex's arms soothed all her fears into the background. She clung to his promise, even as she clung to his body. Just like the night before, every inch of him was pressed to her. Tightly. Her breasts were crushed to his chest, his hips molded to hers. Their thighs brushed together almost sinuously.

"Let's get out of here," he whispered.

Emily gasped for air again when he let her go. Her panic attack was about to be surpassed by an entirely different kind of attack. Alex, on the other hand, looked calm and cool, all his senses trained on the street.

"Looks like I'm kidnapping you once more," he

said, as they left the meager security of the shop doorway.

As she followed him Emily realized the prospect of staying with Alex was not at all unpleasant. Words like "intrigued" and "excited" better described how she felt.

She sighed. The Stockholm Syndrome was a reality.

"I should have tried for it."

"Forget it," Alex snapped, as Emily voiced her new obsession for the hundredth time.

They had no sooner left the embassy area than she had begun her bravado statements. How she could even think it was beyond him. The closeness he'd experienced with her in the doorway was shattered. It was a good thing they'd made it to Tuno's street without incident. And he wasn't thinking of his uncle's soldiers. Emily ought to be grateful he hadn't left her behind.

He steered them toward the alleyway in back of Tuno's home, figuring it would keep prying eyes to a minimum.

"I think you didn't want to try because you're afraid I'll give you away," she said.

This was a tack he didn't like at all. "I won't even dignify that with an answer."

"I bet that's what Nixon said about the eighteen-minute gap on the tape."

"Get in the damn house."

He cursed under his breath as they crossed the small courtyard behind Tuno's apartment. Alex tapped on the sliding glass door more loudly than he'd intended. Emily had gotten under his skin more than he cared to admit.

The door's curtain flipped aside a few inches, then the door was slid open.

"Praise be!" Tuno exclaimed. "Inside! Inside!"

They were in the living room in an instant, and Alex was gratified to see Emily walk in without hesitation. The door closed them into a nether-world, leaving the outside far behind.

"Did anyone see you?" Tuno asked.

"I don't think so," Alex said.

The old man shook his head. "Just after you left, I heard on the radio that your uncle has surrounded all the embassies. I have been terrified that the two of you walked right into a trap."

"We nearly did," Alex said, eyeing Emily sourly.

"I still think I could have made it," she said.

"The hell you could have!" he exclaimed, his anger boiling over.

"I think I'll make some tea," Tuno murmured, and disappeared into the kitchen.

"See?" Emily said. "You've upset the man."

"*I've* upset the man!"

"I can't believe I'm back here," she went on, pacing around the room like a caged animal.

What, he wondered, had happened to the soft creature he'd held in his arms? That moment of closeness had touched him in a way he hadn't expected. Even though he knew it was for her own safety, he still felt guilty as hell for forcing her to stay with him. But why should he care so much? He didn't understand. Maybe it was the Stockholm Syndrome. He wondered if she were feeling any similar effects.

He grinned, imagining her reaction if he asked her.

"What's so funny?" she demanded.

He smothered the grin and shrugged. "Nothing. Just thinking." He decided to try one last time with her. "Emily, this is much more safe for you right now. I'll get you home. I promise. I just need a little time to come up with a plan. Do you think you can put up with this for a while longer?"

"No. But I don't have any choice, do I?"

"No." He smiled. "I knew under the tigress there was a sensible schoolteacher."

She smiled sweetly. "Honey, you ain't seen nothin' yet."

Boy, he hoped not.

He went into the kitchen to help Tuno make tea.

Three

"Got any sevens?"

Emily looked over her cards. "Go fish."

His expression deadpan, Alex rooted through the pile of cards on the dining table. Emily hid a smile of amusement as a real live prince played a children's game with all the concentration of a high-stakes poker player.

She was living with a prince, she thought, still awed by the notion. An honest-to-goodness prince right out of the fairy tales. No one in the Teachers' Room would believe this one. Emily Cooper stolen away by a prince. Heck, even Snow White had had to get stuck in a glass coffin before her Prince Charming showed up.

Realizing what she was doing, she looked away and swallowed back a barnyard curse. She had to stop this constant daydreaming. It wasn't helping.

She had finally calmed down, after the embassy fiasco, realizing that being at Tuno's was better for her—for the moment. But the anxiety to get home was always just under the surface, and growing.

For three days, they had been cooped up here, continually tripping over each other. She wanted desperately to make it one fewer, but Alex wouldn't let her go. The people were still protesting and the embassies were still closed. He wouldn't allow Tuno to go out. Just to keep safe, he'd said. They had to talk in low voices, although the portable radio was turned up to cover any odd sounds. Ever since their trip to the embassy, he was worried someone had seen them coming in or going out and would report it.

The claustrophobia was making all of them a little crazy. Relief came in funny ways, like a game of Go Fish. Good thing she'd put a pack of cards in her flight bag.

"Emily," Alex prompted her.

She looked back at her cards. "Got any aces?"

Alex and Tuno groaned loudly and each handed over one. She smiled and tucked them into her hand, and took out a matching set of four. "Read 'em and weep, boys."

"I think she marks the cards," Alex said, turning his over and looking at the backs.

"I think she counts them," Tuno said, frowning at his own hand.

"I do not!" Emily said indignantly. She pulled the cards out of their hands and started shuffling. "You know the old saying, 'Lucky at cards, unlucky at love.' Well, that's me."

"What were you unlucky about?" Alex asked, eyeing her speculatively.

She shrugged. "Michael Garroty dumped me for Virginia Melanksy in the second grade and I've never recovered." Suddenly she slammed the cards down and jumped up. "I can't stand this anymore! I have to leave. I have to go home. Easter break is over the day after tomorrow, and I have to be there when my children come back to school!"

"Sit down," Alex said.

She glowered at him. "No, I will not sit down! So what if you're some big-shot prince everyone is hot for, you can't make me stay—"

"Emily, please," Tuno said soothingly, as he stood up. "I'll go use the facilities by candlelight. Alexi! Talk to her."

"About what?"

Tuno frowned at him. Emily sat back down and laid her head on the table, feeling numb inside.

Tuno's footsteps faded away. After a long moment a hand began to stroke her hair, tentatively, then more firmly when she didn't flinch. "Emily, you know I would let you go to the embassy if I could. I would take you home myself right now if that were possible. You must be patient. We'll get you home."

"How?" she asked, choking out the word. She raised her head and tried to fight down the panic that had come on so fast.

Alex had no answer to her question.

She slumped in temporary defeat. "I'm sorry for the moment of insanity. I get impulsive sometimes, but it passes like bad gas. Not that there's any good kind." She realized she was babbling like an idiot. "I think I'll go get something to drink. Do you want anything?"

He shook his head.

She went into the kitchen and leaned wearily against the still-defunct refrigerator, closing her eyes. She'd give anything to click some ruby slippers together and chant, "There's no place like home." Hell's bells, she thought. She'd settle for a pair of beat-up sneakers if the suckers worked.

Sensing someone entering the kitchen, she opened her eyes and straightened away from the appliance. It was Alex. Just what she needed, she thought, as an unstoppable warmth flooded through her veins. There was something about him that pulled at her constantly. Her earlier panic was more than just anxiety, and she knew it. Alex had a potent effect on her, one she didn't know how to cope with. Even though she'd been married, Alex roused a fascination in her that she'd never felt for any man. Everything he did captivated her, and at least once every hour she had to remind herself not to stare at him. Maybe it was because he was the only safe haven she had, but she sensed a comforting aura of strength and confidence about him. He made her feel secure, and she tried to tell herself that that was all there was to it. But "secure" was not what she felt when he accidentally touched her hand, or when they bumped into each other as they maneuvered around the small apartment. She felt a conflagration that scared the wits out of her. What made it worse, though, was that Alex seemed to feel nothing at all.

She had to pull herself together and not let him get to her. He might carry all the trappings of a little girl's fairy tale, but that didn't mean she had to respond.

"I'm sorry," he said.

She shrugged. "Like I said, it was just a momentary break in the sanity department. Don't feel bad."

"You're very generous about what happened to you." He moved closer. "I don't know if I could be."

She shrugged again to cover her sudden nervousness. She didn't trust her voice when he was only inches from her.

He leaned forward, almost towering over her. "You've been a good sport about this. Don't worry, Emily. I'll get you home. I promise you that."

He reached out and ran his hand along her arm in encouragement. Emily didn't feel encouraged, though, as a sensual heat spread along her skin, leaving her breathless. Alex Kiros, prince, held a greater danger for her than anything outside the apartment. He seemed to loom above her, and she had the oddest notion he was about to kiss her.

"You'll turn into a frog," she murmured.

"What?" He stepped back, his hand dropping away.

"Nothing." Her cheeks were hot with embarrassment. She didn't know why she should be embarrassed, but she was.

"I thought you were getting a drink," he said.

"I was." She took a small bottle of water and poured a little into a cup, knowing they had to be sparing in their consumption. After taking her two mouthfuls, she set the cup back on the counter. "I think I ought to turn myself in, Alex. I won't tell anyone who you are. Really. Truly. Honestly. They can burn my toes and yank out my fingernails and your name will never pass my lips."

He grimaced. "You're worse than that damn radio, going over and over the same theme. No, Emily."

"The radio has also been saying that if the tourists turn themselves in, they'll be returned to their countries immediately. They're not going to risk detaining any of us for a lot of questions."

"And you believe what the radio says?" He

crossed his arms over his chest, the muscles bulging slightly.

She looked away, as her uncontrollable imagination took flight once more. "How do we know it's not true?"

"You're not finding out," he said in a tone that brooked no argument.

She glared at him for a long moment, then stalked out of the kitchen, through the living room, and into the bedroom. She slammed the door behind her.

Two seconds later, it was flung open and Alex strode in.

"Believe me, I'm grateful for all your wonderful help," she said, then added, "Go away!"

"I'll get you out, dammit! I don't know how, but I will, okay?"

He strode back out and yanked the door shut. She could hear him cursing in the other room.

"Serves him right," she muttered, sitting down on the bed.

"Oh, I don't know," Tuno said as he walked out of the bathroom. "He's not a bad sort. Just bossy. That comes from living in America for so long."

Emily groaned. Everywhere she turned, someone was there. "Can I borrow your closet?"

He raised his eyebrows. "Why?"

"To have a moment's peace."

"You get to sleep in a room alone every night," he pointed out.

"With the door open." Alex could say what he wanted, but that was yet another sign of his lack of trust in her.

"It could be worse," Tuno said. "You could be sleeping in the other room. Alex snores."

She grinned reluctantly. "What makes you think I can't hear him?"

Tuno chuckled. "You are a delight."

"I'm glad someone thinks so."

"He's just worried." Tuno paused. "Emily, it isn't safe for you to go out or turn yourself in. And it isn't safe for him. You don't know his uncle and how he will use him. Florian is rounding up all the relatives to pose with him for a public show of support. Alex, if he is found, will be coerced into participating. For all the boy says he is neutral, he has much honor and will not support his uncle in the coup."

She swallowed. The word "support" conjured up frightening images. "Why didn't Alex tell me that?"

"He probably didn't want to worry you any more than you already are."

She nodded, afraid again to speak. She might cry instead, because she wanted to go home so badly. She hated crying. It made her nose turn red and her mascara run until she looked like a drunk racoon.

Tuno went to the door. "I'll get out of your way. You could use the rest. We won't have any sleep tonight with Alex trying to raise the roof."

The elderly man closed the door gently behind him. Emily flopped back on the bed, tears streaming out of her eyes. All she wanted was to get out of everyone's hair and go home. Why was that so impossible to do?

Feeling selfish, she swiped at her tears. Alex was in a much more dangerous position than she.

If anyone had ever told her that one day she'd meet a handsome prince in an alley, then go to live with him and a retired palace majordomo, she would have sent them back to fortune-telling school.

Clearly, they had missed "Unlikely Predictions and How to Avoid Them, 101."

"A Big Mac, french fries, and a cola."

"A Big Mac, french fries, and a cola," Tuno repeated diligently.

"Now if you go to Burger King, you order a Whopper, french fries, and a cola," Emily lectured. "Let me hear you."

"A Whopper, french fries, and a cola," her student parroted.

"Are you planning to go through every fast-food chain in the States?" Alex asked, smothering his laughter.

"I have to. There are none in Peraco," she said.

"Miracle of miracles." Alex was still chuckling.

"Tuno is learning practical applications so that if he ever gets to visit the States, he'll be well-prepared for the life there," Emily told him, with a no-nonsense look in her eyes.

"I want to be very practical," Tuno said. "I want to experience real American life. Milk shakes . . . Coca-Cola . . . french fries . . . Big Joes . . ."

Emily laughed. "Big Macs, Tuno."

Alex had the distinct feeling the older man was trying to charm Emily for more than a distraction. But Tuno was long past his prime for that sort of thing. Then he looked at Emily, who was clearly delighted in her pupil, and at her pupil, who was clearly delighted in her. He wondered if one's "prime" ever ended, and hated himself for the primitive urges running through him.

He knew he should be concentrating on getting

both of them out of the country. He tried, but Emily was constantly in view, creating her own charming distraction. The way her hair fell along her cheek . . . her knowing grin when she was doing something silly to amuse them all . . . her exuberance . . . the unconscious sensual laziness in her eyes when she first woke up in the morning. He couldn't keep his gaze off her then.

"Alex," she said, drawing his attention. Still filled with his thoughts, he smiled helplessly at her. She went on, "Believe me, I know what Tuno needs. I'm the schoolteacher, remember? Besides, what good does it do Tuno to say, 'The bones are in the basket'?"

"Who says that?" he asks.

"My Greek phrase book." That knowing grin spread across her face. Alex waited in delight as she continued, "I think it's in case you turn into a psychotic killer while on vacation. Then you can make a proper confession: 'Yes, I did it, and the bones are in the basket.' Either that, or you're making soup for dinner."

He grinned back. It was good to see her smiling again. Especially after their fight in the kitchen that morning. He hadn't meant to fight with her, but after she'd snapped, he'd snapped. Being the quintessential diplomat, Tuno never snapped.

As Alex watched her, he acknowledged he wanted to trust her completely. Logic told him she wouldn't say anything about him and no one would try to pry the information out of her. But still he hesitated. He couldn't help it. And maybe hesitant was the healthiest way to be right now. He only hoped she would eventually forgive him for that slight distrust.

She had to. She possessed a vitality that fascinated him. She was down-to-earth compared to the elegant mannequin he'd been briefly married to. Yet put her in a gown and take her to a ball, he had no doubt he'd witness a Pygmalion transformation. What worried him, though, was that his attraction to her, rather than being simple and friendly, was complicated by a powerful lust. He'd nearly kissed her in the kitchen, the desire coming on suddenly and overwhelmingly.

Now was not the time for that, he told himself. He needed no distractions if he was going to get her out of Peraco. The question was how. So far, he'd had no answers.

"Now," he heard Emily say to Tuno, "if you're driving and someone cuts you off, you say, 'Jerk! Where did you learn to drive? Disney World?'"

"Disney World!" Tuno became excited. "What do you say to Mickey Mouse?"

"What's a short guy like you doing inside that oven?" Alex suggested.

Emily glared at him. "Alex, you'll spoil the mystique for Tuno." She turned back to her pupil. "You say, 'What's your preferred stock going for these days?'"

Alex snorted in amusement.

"It's practical," Emily reminded him.

"I'll tell you what else is practical," Tuno said, sitting up. "And that's how to get you two over the border. I just thought of it. I know where to get passports—"

"They're stopping everybody," Alex interrupted.

"Not the local Greeks or Turks who cross over for work, I'll bet." Tuno paused. "Well, maybe at the moment, but, Alex, you don't have to cross at the checkpoints. And with false identity papers, you and Emily won't be any different from any other locals if you're stopped."

Alex frowned. Here he was, right in the middle of chaos, upholding familial duty and appearance, a job he didn't relish, and the sooner he got out the better. Yet he hesitated. "I don't know."

"I do. And I know someone who can get the papers for you," Tuno said, rising from his chair. "He's a former Ministry manager and he doesn't live far from here. I will go see him now."

Tuno was out the sliding glass doors before Alex could stop him.

"Tuno!" he shouted as much as a whisper would allow. "Tuno, dammit!"

But the man was gone.

Alex turned his annoyance on Emily, who was wide-eyed. But before he could speak, the lights came on.

"Looks like they finally found the plug," she said.

Alex nodded. Somehow the reconnection of a vital service boded more ill than good. He could only wait for Tuno to come back. Fury and frustration shot through him at the thought of his friend endangering himself.

Emily got up and began to pace the room. He watched her, unable not to. She walked with an unconscious grace. Her sweater revealed and yet softened the curves of her body, and her jeans molded to her hips and thighs in a way his hands longed to. Her hair was pulled back in the ever-present ponytail, and he itched to take out the barrette and feel the dark strands wrap around his fingers, as they had this morning when she'd exploded in anger. She was becoming more and more like a caged animal. He wanted to set her free, but he had his doubts that Tuno's Greek disguise was the way.

"Do you think we could pose as Greek locals?" she asked.

"Sure. You can tell the guards the bones are in the basket right before they drag us away."

"You don't have to be sarcastic," she said, stopping to face him, her hands on her hips.

"I wasn't being sarcastic. I was being sardonic."

"I'm glad you cleared that up for me, otherwise I would have gone through life confused." She paused. "By the way, that was sarcasm."

"No kidding." He got up and began to turn off the lights, since it was still daylight.

"I would think you'd want to go," she said. "Especially since your uncle wants to use you the way he does."

He rounded on her. "How the hell do you know that?"

"Tuno told me. We've both got to leave, and maybe this is the way."

"Why are you so desperate to get home? Is there a man waiting?"

The words had no sooner popped out of his mouth than he wished them back. They revealed too well that he was beginning to care about her.

She didn't seem to notice, though. "No man." She sniffed in disdain. "Just brothers. Five of them, who'll probably come over here and tear this place apart if I'm not home soon."

"I suppose you mean they'll tear me apart."

She smiled briefly. "Probably. I don't understand you, Alex. Why are you acting like this is the worst idea since Napoleon decided to take on Waterloo?"

"Because I think it might be."

"You aren't giving it a chance. I think we should go. And, dammit, if you won't, I will!"

"No!"

"Yes!"

Something exploded inside him. He reached out and dragged her against him, then lowered his mouth to hers in a fiery kiss. She made a noise of protest in the back of her throat, but he paid no attention to it, wanting only to taste the sweetness of her, to take for himself.

For just a moment her lips softened under his. For just a moment she seemed willing to take for herself. Then she pushed at him and he let her go, realizing what he was doing. Stepping back, he ran his hand through his hair in complete frustration. "Sorry."

She nodded, turning away from him. Her face was white.

"It was my moment of insanity," he added lamely.

She nodded again. "We all have them."

"That's the truth," he muttered.

The moments drew out into long minutes. The tension in the room was so high, Alex could almost touch it. As they sat on opposite sides of the small room, studiously not looking at each other, he found himself fighting the overwhelming urge to kiss her again, to kiss her so thoroughly, she wouldn't pull away from him . . .

Tuno finally returned, looking extremely pleased with himself. "I saw my friend. He will begin to work on what he thinks is my little problem. I will have to get pictures of you to him. I'll do that tonight. Oh, and he also told me that some of the army units are defecting over to the population . . ." His voice trailed away as he sensed the tension in the room. "Is anything wrong?"

Alex shrugged. "The lights came back on."

"Yes, I know. My friend says the papers will take a while. It will be difficult, but not impossible. You and Emily will go out as man and wife."

A tiny squeak came from Emily. Alex tightened his jaw, but said nothing. He was afraid to.

"It's a good disguise," Tuno added. The talk was normal, but his curious gaze went from one to the other. "They won't be looking for you with a woman, Alex. And Emily, you will have protection and someone who can speak Greek, not just the 'bones in the basket' kind."

Emily looked as if she were about to be stuck with an ax murderer, and Alex really couldn't blame her. After all, his actions so far hadn't encouraged her trust.

"So, Emily. Alex. What do you think of my plan?" Tuno asked.

Emily smiled sweetly. "I think it's wonderful. Excuse me, please. I feel like I'm going to be sick."

She walked into the bedroom and closed the door behind her.

Tuno turned to him. "I leave you alone with her for fifteen minutes and she's ill to her stomach. What did you do?"

Alex sighed. It was going to be a long coup.

That night Emily listened to Alex's loud, even snoring, then slowly and carefully got out of the bed.

The door between the bedroom and living room was open as usual, but where the men slept, they could only see the middle portion of the room. She had deliberately gotten out on the side that faced the bathroom.

She couldn't take being cramped up anymore. Her family was probably worried sick about her, maybe even wondering if she was dead. Her parents must be frantic, especially her mother, who tended to treat her five sons and one daughter like chicks who couldn't find their way out of a paper bag. Emily swallowed back a lump of tears at the thought of the children in her class. This would be traumatic for them. She had to let them know she was all right.

She had to go home. Panic welled up inside her at the thought that she'd never get there. She *had* to go home.

No matter what Tuno and Alex said, she'd be better off turning herself in. They *were* sending people home; they couldn't make that kind of public promise without following through. And even though Alex would never believe her, she wouldn't tell anyone anything about him. She knew she was completely trustworthy and that was enough. Besides, Alex was trouble.

That kiss . . . it had scared her to death. Never had anything curled her toes like that. That she had managed to push him away was a miracle. She refused to think about anything else concerning him. The longer she was exposed to this attractive Prince-in-Trouble, the more she wanted to be Cinderella. The Stockholm Syndrome was real. It was safer for all if she tried her own luck again, because no way, *no way,* was she going anywhere as his "wife." The thought froze her blood right in her veins. She didn't know why it did, and she didn't want to know. She only knew it was a bad idea.

She slipped on her sneakers and pulled her jacket out of her flight bag. Her stomach tightened as the material scraped against the zipper. It sounded like Stanni's machine gun at full blast.

She closed the bag and slipped the strap over her head. Glancing at the door, she wondered if she could sneak through the living room without arousing the men. She decided not to try and, flattening onto her stomach, she crawled under the bed. Her head bumped on the steel side bar, and her hair caught in the box spring. She stiffened, fear running like ice water through her, as her hand encountered a couple of soft lumps. They turned out to be a pair of Turkish carpet slippers.

She let out her breath slowly and pulled herself the rest of the way under the bed.

Still on her belly, she scooted quietly across the rug, then stood up near the window. She listened for any unusual sounds from the other room. Nothing. A more insidious fear slipped along her insides as she faced the window. She prayed it wouldn't make a noise, and put her hand on the catch, unlocking it. She raised the sash . . .

"Meow."

Emily froze, her heart pounding so hard, she thought it would burst right out of her chest. Nothing happened. No hand clamped onto her shoulder and spun her around. No shot in the dark. Nothing. She realized the noise was a cat crying out in the alley and forced herself to calm down, then raised the sash a few more inches.

"Meow."

She whipped back the heavy curtains and stuck her head out the window. There, huddled against the side of the building directly under the window, was a small cat. It looked up at her and meowed again. She reached down and picked it up, wanting only to muzzle those damn cries that sounded louder than Big Ben announcing the hours to all of London.

But her hands closed around bedraggled fur covering prominent ribs. The poor little thing felt about to break apart. Miraculously, the creature began to purr.

With great care, Emily lifted the cat to her chest and ducked back inside the window. Not only was the cat thin, she was also heavily pregnant.

"Going somewhere?"

She whirled around to find Alex standing inside the bedroom, the door closed behind him.

Her escape plan had just hit a snag.

Four

Alex watched Emily soothe the struggling cat she held, fury clouding his vision. She stood so casually in front of him, as if she'd done nothing wrong. The cat relaxed back in her arms and purred.

"You're supposed to be out there snoring."

Of all the things she could have said, he'd never expected that. He could feel his jaw dropping in his astonishment. He clamped it closed. "I don't snore! That's Tuno!"

"Oh."

He glared at her. "You didn't answer my question."

"Yes, I was going somewhere," she said finally. "Home."

Anger and bitterness boiled over inside him. An odd noise had awakened him and he'd seen the empty bed through the doorway. Something had urged him to investigate. Now he was glad he had. "Didn't you listen to what I said before?"

"Yes, I listened," she snapped. She was like a

wraith in the dark. "I'm sorry you don't think I'm trustworthy with who and where you are. But I know I am. Look, if they've publicly promised to send all tourists home immediately, then they have to follow through on that. The whole world is watching. I think it's more foolish for me not to try. My family must think I'm dead. I can't take it!" Her voice rose with her anxiety. "I've got to get word to them that I'm okay."

He strode over to her, wanting to strangle her. It scared him half to death to think of her wandering alone on the streets. "Don't you know that just by hanging out the window you could have already compromised us? Endangered Tuno? Doesn't it occur to you that my uncle knows who Tuno is and he's having him watched in case any of the family shows up?"

She stared at him for a long moment. "It did occur to me . . . but I just wanted to silence the cat."

The cat made a purry meow and butted its head against her chin.

"Here, give it to me." Alex held out his hands. "*I'll* put it out, and then we'll get to the bottom of this."

She turned away, holding the cat even tighter. "No. She's starving . . . and pregnant."

He looked heavenward. "We can't keep it, Emily."

She turned back. "Yes we can. It won't eat much. I'll give it some of my portion. Let me go and she can have all of mine."

He pulled at his hair, realizing the conversation had turned from confrontation to cats.

"I have to go home!" she staggered over to the bed and sat down. The cat hopped out of her arms, and Emily covered her face with her hands and began to cry. Great, gulping sobs. "Why can't anyone understand? I'm tired and I just want to go home!"

Something in her voice tugged at his sympathies. He'd never heard a simple plea sound so genuine. All the frustration and fear inside her was finally spilling out. He sat down next to her. "I'm sorry I was angry. But you were crawling out the window, dammit!"

"I was getting the cat."

"Right." He sighed as she burst into fresh tears. Patting her on the back, he said, "I wish I could let you go, Emily. But think of Tuno. His punishment will be severe for harboring me."

"And you don't trust me not to tell."

"I can't afford to."

She slumped. He realized he'd hurt her, and wished he didn't have to.

"Did you ever think that you could say something innocently that would bring them down on us?" he asked, rubbing her back with slow circular strokes. The cat, sensing the fight was over, settled on the bed, purring loudly.

Emily raised her head. He couldn't see more than the shape of her face in the darkness, but he could sense her surprised expression. "I never would betray you."

"You would never mean to. But what happens when you go home and get interviewed for the papers? And you will. Or *People* magazine? One accidental slip and Tuno will pay. He's risking enough already."

"I suppose I'm the most vulnerable of all," she admitted. "I have had the overwhelming urge to tell everyone in the Teachers' Room back home."

He chuckled. "The light bulb finally went off."

"It works occasionally." She glanced away. "With them calling for the tourists to come in from the cold, you know it will be worse if I'm caught here with Tuno."

"You're small cheese, Emily, compared to me. But I have nowhere to go, and it eats at me to know Tuno could be harshly punished because of me. He—he was like a father to me."

More than his own at times, Alex thought, remembering his parents' global wanderings. A lonely only child, he had been left with a grandfather who'd had no time for him, odd aunts and uncles, and sadistic older cousins. Tuno had come upon him at the age of five, tied up against a pillar in the back corner of the vast cellar for nearly twelve hours. It had been the start of a beautiful, life-saving relationship. Tuno's normalcy had helped foster his own determination to make a stable life for himself outside the family.

But he was more concerned for Emily's safety than even for Tuno's. Tuno knew what could happen. Emily didn't.

"Maybe we ought to hightail it out of here, Greek passports or no," she suggested, amusement in her tone.

"Maybe."

She sighed. "I suppose I'm stuck."

"And I'm stuck with you."

"Tuno is right about both of us going together. I'll help you to get out, Alex." She groaned. "I'll probably regret that."

He smiled. "Well, I guess I appreciate it. Does that make it even?"

She nodded, laughing.

They sat quietly, both lost in thought, though

Alex still rubbed her back. It comforted him just to touch her.

His hand slowly circled the indentation of her waist, the smooth long line of her spine, the delicate curve of her shoulder. Her body was so close to his. He could smell her perfume, light yet clean. No heavy, musk-laden scent that offended rather than enticed.

"Ah . . . Alex?"

"Mmmm?" He turned his face into her hair, the strands like fine silken threads against his roughened cheek.

"I'm feeling much better now."

"Me too."

She leaned away, looking up at him to speak. He did the most natural thing in the world. He kissed her.

Her mouth was soft and lush. His desire had risen too fast that afternoon for him to savor her, and he did so now. It seemed incongruous to find anything gentle in these times, yet her lips more than met that description. He shifted to find more of the softness, rubbing his tongue along the curve of her lower lip. She made a funny sound in the back of her throat, then relaxed against him.

He tightened his arm around her and pulled her fully into the kiss. It was sweeter this time, and all the more intoxicating. Their tongues mated and twisted and twined together in leisurely exploration. Her mouth was velvet fire under his, revealing a passion he would never have expected a kindergarten teacher to possess. Her breasts were pressed against his chest, her hands braced on his arms, the nails digging in slightly with a pleasure-pain that only added to the heat simmering along his veins. It was heady and seductive, and he wanted to forget everything except the feel of her. He wanted to explore every inch of her, to find out if the satisfaction would match the need. The bed beckoned behind him . . .

Emily pulled away, her breath coming in short gasps.

"Well," she said. "You didn't turn into a frog."

"Hardly." He straightened, realizing how foolish he'd been. The last thing he needed was Emily Cooper becoming more of a complication than she was. "And you didn't turn into a princess."

He'd wanted to say something light, but the moment the words left his mouth, he knew they weren't it.

"The magic's gone," she said, rising from the bed and heading for the door. "I suppose I better get something for the cat. She's starving, poor thing."

"Emily."

She turned. Alex wanted to say something about the kiss, something that would take away any sting to his words. "We can't keep the cat."

"We can't send it out there again!" she exclaimed. "It's starving and homeless and pregnant."

"There's a coup going on—"

"I'm well aware of the coup. But that doesn't mean we have to turn into savages." She straightened defiantly. "I will take care of the cat, and she will not get in your way. But if I stay, she stays."

Alex rose. "All right, dammit! But keep her out of my way."

"Fine." She walked to the door.

"Where are you going?"

"To get food for the cat."

"Don't forget water."

"Right."

She practically sailed out the door. Certainly, she sailed past Tuno without a word. He stared expectantly at Alex.

"She's feeding the cat," he said.

"The cat!"

"The cat," Alex said firmly. "It was crying outside the window and drawing attention here. Besides, we're not savages to leave it to starve. Emily will give it a portion of her food. So will I."

The words made him feel good.

"And mine too," Tuno said, sighing. "It's going to be a very fat cat."

"Thank you, gentlemen," Emily said, pushing past them. She held a small bowl in each hand. "Blanche DuBois thanks you as well. And so will her kittens after they're born."

Tuno groaned. He turned away from the door and closed it. Emily set the bowls on the floor. The cat hopped down, sauntered over, and sniffed the food. Despite her obvious hunger, she began to eat delicately.

Alex turned to Emily. "Blanche DuBois?"

"She depends on the kindness of strangers," Emily drawled, then shrugged. "I didn't give her too much food. I was afraid she'd be sick if I did."

Alex shook his head. He'd lost the battle of the cat, and he knew it. He'd also lost the battle of the Great Escape to Greece. He didn't know how, but he had. Maybe he ought to send Emily against his uncle Florian.

The man would never know what hit him.

"You didn't have to sleep across the bedroom threshold," Emily told Alex.

He smiled benignly. "It was my pleasure."

She turned away, feeling her face flush at the sensual tone of his voice. Memories of the kiss they'd shared washed through her like a fine wine, and she could taste him on her mouth all over again. For a brief moment she wondered if he'd also had that all-encompassing feeling of being swept away.

Get out of the fairy tale and get your feet on the ground, Emily Cooper, she mentally lectured. It had just been a kiss of comfort. He was a prince, a sophisticated man. What interest could she ever generate, except a passing one?

She faced him again, determined to pretend nothing had happened the night before. "It was embarrassing to have you . . . like that across the doorway. Suppose someone got up in the middle of the night. They'd trip over you."

He grinned. "That's the point."

She grit her back teeth together for the count of five, then said, "Look, I won't try to go out on my own again, okay?"

"Good." He rolled up the blanket he'd been using and set it next to the door.

Emily stared at it. "You're not sleeping there again tonight."

He straightened and leaned against the door-jamb. "Then I'll sleep *inside* the room."

She hadn't slept at all with him just on the threshold. Inside would make her insane. This was punishment for trying to escape, she thought. Damn that cat. Thanks to Blanche, Alex was more determined than ever to keep her there. If she were going to be forced to continue in this impossible situation, and it looked as if she were, then she wanted to do it in reasonable harmony. Otherwise she wouldn't survive.

"Fine," she said. "On the threshold. I get the message, Alex. All of it."

"I'm not trying to insult you—"

"And you're doing a lousy job of it." She smiled as insincerely as possible. Feeling a stabbing pinch on her arm, she slapped at the spot. It was a flea. She sighed. "I was afraid of that. Blanche is carrying more than kittens. She's got fleas."

Alex groaned. "Wonderful. Now we'll all get them."

"Not necessarily." She walked over to her flight bag and rummaged inside until she found what she wanted. She pulled out a bottle with a thick mint-green liquid inside. "Skin So Right from Avalon Cosmetics. It'll make your skin clear and soft in seven days . . . and kill every flea within a hundred yards in the process."

He gaped at her. "You're kidding."

"Nope. Nobody's quite sure why, but it does, although I often wonder what it's really doing to my skin."

"Do you think it'll hurt the kittens?"

"I don't think so. She's far enough along that they're fully formed. In fact, she feels very near delivery to me." Emily had to admit she was touched by his concern, yet it left her oddly uncomfortable. She was glad he hadn't ventured inside the room.

"How do you know about the kittens?" he asked.

"I was raised on a boarding horse farm. We had cats for the barn. You kinda get to know."

Oh, brother, she thought, embarrassment heating her cheeks again. That had sounded wonderfully intelligent. *You kinda get to know.*

All he said was, "Oh."

She went on, determined to sound a little brighter. "The fleas will be worse after they're born. Blanche isn't lactating yet, so this is about the safest time as far as the chemicals are concerned."

"This better work then," Alex said, and his expression was grim.

"In the bathroom."

She got Blanche, who was curled up on the bed, asleep. Alex had already set the stopper in the sink and was running water into the bowl. When he finished, she handed him the cat, who began to purr contentedly. Emily wet one of Tuno's washcloths—made of thick, luxuriant terry cloth, it no doubt was part of an extremely expensive set of bath towels—then poured some of the Skin So Right onto the cloth.

"Okay," she said. "Put her in."

He lowered Blanche toward the water. All four legs splayed out in an attempt to avoid it. The cat yowled with indignation the moment her paws touched wetness. Alex managed to get her legs in, and Emily began to scrub the cat with the cloth, banding the neck first.

Blanche fussed and struggled and hissed and moaned, while Alex grappled and cursed. Grinning at the antics of both, Emily scrubbed away, working as quickly as possible.

"Don't hurt her," she warned.

"Don't hurt her!" he yelped. "She's clawed me in six different places already!"

"Stop being a baby, Alex."

"A baby!" He grumbled in Peracan under his

breath. Emily had a feeling she didn't want a translation.

Blanche gave up the fight fairly quickly, clearly sensing that if she endured the torture, it would stop sooner. Her eyes, though, were squeezed shut and her ears were laid flat against her wet head in unhappiness. Alex relaxed his grip, although it had been gentle from the first. His hands moved away from whatever spot Emily needed to work on without her having to tell him. It was rather like a *pas de deux*, she thought. She was also uncomfortably aware of him standing so close to her, their arms rubbing along each other, her elbow and shoulder literally over his as they worked. His breath was in her hair, skittering along the edge of her awareness. The scent of man and mint filled her nostrils.

Fleas jumped on them in an effort to get away from death by cleansing lotion. Emily ran her soapy hands down Alex's bare arms to swipe off the critters and protect him. His muscles were corded and hard, like tempered steel. She stifled a moan of pleasure at the sensuousness of cool liquid and warm flesh. It was only the addition of wet cat that kept her from flinging herself at him. Finally, Blanche was scrubbed as clean as Emily could get her.

"It'll have to do," she muttered. She opened the sink stopper, adding, "Okay, let's rinse her down."

"Right." His voice sounded oddly hoarse, and he didn't move.

Emily frowned, but began running fresh water into the sink. Blanche bucked and protested loudly. Emily brushed off the excess water, then grabbed a towel and wrapped the cat in it. She crooned a silly song as she rubbed Blanche's fur dry. The cat actually began to purr.

"It doesn't take much to make her happy," Alex said.

Emily chuckled. "She's probably just grateful it's all over."

She set Blanche on the floor. With admirable dignity, the wet, bedraggled cat sauntered out of the bathroom.

"Oh, brother," Emily said. "If that isn't Blanche DuBois, then I don't know who is."

She turned back to Alex to see his reaction to the cat. He wasn't amused. Instead, he was staring at her breasts. She realized her shirt was wet from holding the cat, the opaque cotton knit now a revealing veil from neck to waist. Her bra, made of thin Lycra, might as well have been nonexistent. Heat flushed her cheeks, and she wanted to cross her arms over her chest. But that would acknowledge the sensual awareness between them.

His gaze finally moved to her face. Emily glanced elsewhere . . . and cursed herself for the giveaway.

"About the kiss," he began.

"It was just a kiss," she said lightly. She was determined to take it lightly. She patted his arm, just as she would one of her brothers. "Alex, relax. There was nothing to it but cramped quarters and a momentary surge of hormones. No big deal." She forced herself to laugh. "Besides, I've been kissed by a prince before."

Prince Charming was in the annual kindergarten production of *Snow White*. Last year Jason Taylor, in feathered hat and cape, had given her a wet, sloppy kiss after the show. That qualified as a prince to her.

Alex stared at her, clearly not expecting this kind of reaction from her. Good, she thought, and turned around to leave the room. She only hoped she could muster as much dignity as Blanche had.

"I could hear you breathing in the night."

Emily froze in mid-stride, her jaw clenched against the sudden welling of trepidation inside her. All night she had forced herself to lie still, to not show any restlessness at his proximity. She had counted to a thousand and gone over curricula for the next five years in an effort to find sleep. But he had heard her breathing.

Slowly, she turned around. "We all breathe, Alex."

"Not like you."

His face was hard, almost like stone, and expressionless. Yet his words were filled with more sexuality than she'd ever encountered before.

"We all breathe," she repeated, in an attempt to keep her control.

He reached out and touched her cheek. "Not like you."

He brushed past her and left the room.

Emily wanted to scream, to dive through the window and run for her life. She would lose more of herself, never to be regained, if she gave in to the emotions riding her. Last night's panic was nothing compared to this.

Tuno was late.

Alex paced the small apartment, cursing under his breath. He never should have let the man go.

"Your pacing like a caged bear is not going to bring him back any quicker," Emily said, stroking the cat who sat on her lap.

"It makes me feel better." He wondered how she could be so calm. Only one light was lit, giving the dark room a ghostly illumination. It was all they dared do, even with the heavy curtains pulled across the windows.

He admitted that while one half of him was worried about Tuno, the other half was all too aware of just himself and Emily alone in the apartment. It was a temptation he could barely endure, and he didn't trust himself not to give in to it. Their kiss had held an honesty that had taken him by surprise, honest passion and honest need. She felt the same attraction he did, he knew it. He shouldn't have kissed her, though. Things had been complicated enough before. But desire had been given its first freedom, and the door that should have been kept closed had been opened. It had taken every ounce of his control to only stare at her breasts this morning. Her nipples had been taut with dampness. Then they had tightened with something more. He'd wanted so much to touch them . . . taste them . . . to rub his tongue against the sensitive nub and feel Emily Cooper, kindergarten teacher, shake off the bonds to her passion.

Alex mentally shut down the picture in his mind, knowing it was only digging him in deeper with her. In trying to tell her so earlier, he'd only made things worse. At least there was something he could do now.

He walked over to her and touched her hair. He smiled when she looked up at him. "Emily, I know this hasn't been easy for you, all alone in a strange country that's in trouble. You've been wonderful for the past four days, and your caring and concern have helped to lighten them for me and Tuno."

She swallowed visibly, and her hoarse voice betrayed her emotions. "Well, I'm glad you all appreciated the card games and English lessons."

"Blanche, we're not so sure about yet."

She laughed and ruffled the cat's fur.

A soft knock came at the front door. They stared at it. There were three more raps, then two, then three.

Alex breathed a sigh of relief. "Tuno."

He went to the door and opened it. Tuno slipped in. He looked white as a sheet. To Alex's surprise, Stanni slipped in after the older man.

"Stanni!"

The young man grinned. "I told you I would be back."

"What's happened?" Alex asked.

"I've got the papers and met with Stanni, that's what took so long," Tuno said, pulling the passports out of his coat. His eyes were wide with fear . . . and something else. He glanced beyond Alex, then back. "I've also got some more food. I was lucky to meet up with a food store manager I know, who has a hoarded supply." He stepped around Alex. "Emily, I even have cat food."

"Wonderful!" She smiled at Tuno and rubbed the cat under its chin. "You're living up to your namesake with a vengeance, Blanche."

"And Mr. Micawber strikes again too," Alex said, keeping his tone light. Something was wrong. He could almost taste it.

"Here." Tuno thrust out the pillowcase he held, and Alex took it from him. It was heavy with his booty. "Take it into the kitchen, boy. I've done enough for one night."

As Alex walked into the kitchen, he could hear Stanni greeting Emily. Once away from other eyes, he immediately opened the bag, positive that whatever had distressed Tuno was inside it. He stared at the contents—bottles of water, canned goods, fruit that was overripe but still edible, cereals and crackers, tinned sardines, and the promised cat food. There was nothing out of the ordinary.

Tuno came into the kitchen a minute later, Stanni right behind him.

"What is it?" Alex asked, pointing to the booty.

"Food." The old man was excited and fearful at the same time. He glanced back at the doorway, then whispered, "Stanni, show him."

Turning his body so Emily couldn't see if she walked past the doorway, Stanni reached inside his shirt and pulled out a large blue velvet bag. He laid it in Alex's hands.

"Stanni met with Pieter," Tuno explained. "A complication."

Pieter was another trusted retainer of the palace. Alex watched as Stanni loosened the drawstrings and pushed back the velvet. Thin bands of burnished gold and silver twined in a circlet, the workmanship ancient and exquisite. A large ruby on a pendant, encased in gold filigree, lay inside the circlet, along with a plain golden orb topped with a diamond cross.

Alex swallowed back a lump of pure fear as he stared at the crown jewels of Peraco. "Complication" was an understatement.

Tuno had brought back a mess.

Five

"If there is no crown, there is no coronation," Tuno said softly.

Alex snapped his head up to stare at the older man. Shock and confusion jumbled through his mind. The prettily fashioned lumps he held somehow didn't look like the vitally important artifacts they were. "What . . . where did you get them?"

"Pieter," Tuno said.

"But how . . . ?"

"He was brilliant," Stanni said, grinning at Alex. "In all the excitement, nobody thought of them, I guess. Clearly, they didn't go with your aunt when she fled."

"I don't think Florian has given them a thought since," Tuno added. "Why would he? But Pieter did, and he's thought of how a coronation can't take place without them. And without the crown and the pendant and the scepter, how can Florian be crowned? He can't—"

"But what are we supposed to do with them?" Alex interrupted.

"Take them out of the country when you and Emily go," Tuno answered.

Alex immediately dumped them back onto Tuno who, startled, nearly dropped them.

"Take them out!" Alex exclaimed, horrified by the thought. "I can't take them out!"

"Of course you can," Stanni said. "Alex, you're the only one who can do it."

"No." Alex backed away toward the kitchen entrance. "I told you I wasn't involved in any of this, and I'm not about to be. I'm just a computer company owner here on a job!"

"You're a prince of the House of Kiros," Tuno said, as he and Stanni stalked him. "It is your duty, Alex, to take them to your aunt. You can do nothing else, and if you search your heart, you will know it's true."

"Pieter has risked everything to get them out of the palace," Stanni added, hammering home. "You remember gentle Pieter, Alex. How can you do less than he?"

Alex grit his teeth together. How *could* he do less? They had the false identity papers now—not that they'd be much good if he and Emily were caught. Emily spoke no Greek and could fool no one, and he could be recognized. The risks were already tremendous, and now . . . now they were beyond comprehension.

"Dammit," he said, "I'm just here to put in a computer system for the government. I can't smuggle crown jewels out of Peraco. I can't."

Tuno fixed him with a hard stare. "You know you must, boy. There is no one else who can."

Frustrated, Alex spun on his heel and walked out of the kitchen. He couldn't take the crown jewels out of the country. Why would anyone expect him to? He had no experience in furtive missions. This was a job for James Bond. And he would not get involved with the crazy family squabbles. He'd be as nuts as the rest of them if he did. Let one of the other family members take them out . . .

His brain reminded him that there wasn't any-one left who was capable of rescuing the throne from his ambitious uncle. Everyone had already fled Peraco's troubles.

"So when do we feast?"

"Wha . . ." Alex realized he had walked right past Emily without noticing her. Stolen crown jewels may have their advantages, after all. They'd distract him from his growing desire for her.

"Ahhh . . ." He cleared his throat and tried to gather some coherent thoughts. Emily gazed at him expectantly. He felt like a kindergartner asked why he'd let the class hamster out of its cage. "Well, I expect Tuno's tired tonight."

"I thought maybe you were whipping up some-thing. You were in there a long time."

He shrugged. "Just the latest news—"

"Really!" Excitement rang in her voice. "What news? What's going on in the real world?"

Alex rubbed his forehead in a desperate attempt to bring anything into his brain that remotely sounded like news. "The world's protesting my uncle's actions."

"That's it? That's not news."

"The U.N. is drawing up resolutions," Stanni said, emerging from the kitchen. Alex sighed in relief. Stanni added, "That's really going to put the pressure on Florian."

"Why didn't you tell me that?" Emily asked Alex.

"Because he worries too much," Tuno said from behind Stanni. "And he was fussing over me. It's embarrassing at my age to have a mother hen."

Emily grinned. "I always thought Alex was fussy."

"Nobody fusses worse than you," Alex said, grateful for the diversion. "Look at that cat."

Blanche's shining fur and just-swallowed-a-canary look spoke for themselves.

"If you will excuse me," Tuno murmured, heading for the bedroom.

Emily knew he meant to use the "facilities," and she admired his discretion. In fact, everyone was acting nice and casual about the way they'd disappeared into and reappeared from the kitchen. She wasn't fooled, though. Alex's face had been ashen. Something had happened. Something they didn't want her to know about.

Because they couldn't trust her.

Alex sat down beside her on the sofa, and she forced herself not to stiffen with awareness. Reasonable harmony, her mind chanted like a mantra. The last thing she felt, however, was any sort of harmony as he began to pet the cat, the back of his fingers brushing her stomach as he did. A sizzling warmth stroked along her skin, and she tensed her muscles against it. She didn't dare do more. She didn't want anyone to know Alex affected her. It would be nice if Alex didn't know either, but she had a feeling he did.

"I'm going to bed," she announced the moment Tuno came out of the bedroom. She set Blanche on Alex's lap and walked into the bedroom, wanting badly to slam the door behind her. Unfortunately, that would put everyone in an uproar. Instead, she grabbed pillows and bedclothes and dumped them on the floor next to the bed, on the side away from prying eyes. Kneeling, she yanked the covers around, mumbling vindictives under her breath. She wondered what the penalty was for killing a prince. It would be worth it. And she deserved some satisfaction out of all this.

Somehow, some way, she would see Alex give her complete trust and acknowledge it in front of everyone.

Settling down in her makeshift bed, Emily smiled as a thought occurred to her. She was getting a small revenge at the moment. With her going to bed early, none of the men could use the bathroom.

Ah, life was sweet.

Several hours later, Emily awoke to find Blanche sitting on her chest, crying piteously.

"What's wrong?" She rubbed her eyes, trying to force the sleep from them.

Blanche crawled off her and stood stock-still, panting, for one long minute.

"Uh-oh," Emily muttered as the cat cried again.

"What is it?" Alex whispered from the doorway. He sounded wide-awake.

"It's Blanche. I think she's in labor."

"Now?"

"Yes, now." Blanche stopped crying and panted again. Watching the little creature, Emily said, "I think she's in hard labor. The kittens aren't far away."

"What do we do?" She could hear him crawling closer. The cat went to him and cried her story again.

"Let nature take its course," Emily replied.

"Shouldn't we boil water or something? Rip up sheets? That's what they do in the movies."

"The sheets I can understand, to wrap the baby in." Emily couldn't help grinning. The prince was in a panic over a cat. "But, Alex, what will we do with the hot water?"

"I don't know."

"Me neither. I never could figure that out. Maybe the helpers are supposed to dip their hands in to sterilize them. That must hurt. Surely they didn't dip the mother in to sterilize her. What a horrifying thought—"

"Emily, dammit! What do we do?" His desperation was tangible in the darkness as Blanche panted and cried again.

"What's wrong?" Tuno asked from the doorway.

"Blanche is having her kittens now," Emily said.

Two groans alerted her to another presence.

"Stanni?"

"Yes. I'm here."

"He stayed because of the curfew," Alex explained.

"Blanche, you have an audience." Emily stroked the cat to soothe her. Blanche cried again. "An Academy Award performance in the making."

Blaring sirens erupted.

"What is it?" Emily yelled, jumping in fright. They all did. In sheer terror, Blanche scooted under the bed, temporarily ignoring nature's progress. The sirens didn't pass on. Instead they screamed at the top of their mechanical lungs without fading.

"It's on this street," Alex said over the noise. "Tuno, can we check this somehow?"

"I will try the door's peephole."

"Maybe he shouldn't," Emily said, nearly shouting to be heard.

"Carefully," Alex warned the older man.

Tuno moved away. A minute crawled by while they waited. Blanche cried three times from under the bed.

Emily could feel trickles of sweat rolling down her temples. Her nails were digging into the rug. Her brain yelled "RUN!" and yet her body wouldn't move.

"Alex." It was Tuno's voice. "They're on the other side of the street, knocking on several doors. I think it's a house-to-house search of some kind."

"Omigod," Emily whimpered. They would all be caught. Images of what would happen to them raced through her mind, her imagination running away with itself.

"We'll have to go out the back," Alex said. "Stanni, get food from the kitchen, but leave enough of what a normal individual would hoard. They must know who Tuno is and that he lives alone. Let's make them think he's had no visitors. Emily, get rid of all the bed things in the living room. Put them in closets or something, anywhere. Let's move."

Everyone did, like silent mice in an empty church. After grabbing up the men's bedclothes, Emily knelt down at the edge of the bed. "Blanche, come on, sweetheart—"

"We can't take the cat!"

Emily turned at Alex's voice. He was standing by the bedroom closet with Tuno. "We can't leave her. Alex, please!"

He strode over and reached down, pulling her to her feet and tearing the sheets and blankets out of her arms. She felt like a rag doll in his grip. His voice was the harshest and most desperate she had ever heard. "We can't take her, Emily, and that's final!"

"But—!"

"Alex, go," Tuno ordered. "Emily, don't worry. *I'll* take care of Blanche."

Emily suddenly gasped as she realized that whoever was searching the houses had come because she'd been seen the night she'd rescued Blanche. She's caused this and put Tuno in trouble. "You have to come with us now," she said to him.

"I have no fake papers, and I would only slow you down anyway." He paused. "Someone must stay and misdirect them."

"Tuno—"

"No. Now go!"

Alex turned, still holding her, but she dug her heels in. She knew Tuno had never planned to go with them, but she couldn't leave him behind to this. "Alex! You can't leave him!"

"Yes he can," Tuno said. "He knows he must."

"He'll be safe after we're gone, Emily," Alex said.

"No!"

"Yes!" His patience gone, he dragged her along with him, his hand like a band of iron on her arm. Emily stumbled over her flight bag and snatched it up again, just as she had the first time they met. She was so scared, her teeth were chattering. Half of her knew Alex and Stanni had to leave and she with them, while the other half wanted desperately to stay in this safe haven. The Stockholm Syndrome was looking better and better by the second.

"Alex, wait."

He halted at Tuno's request. "What?"

"Here." The man put something in Alex's hand. "The keys to my car. The apartment garages are down at the end of the alley. Mine's the seventh from the right. I think the tank is full."

"Thanks." Alex's voice held so much gratitude, Emily could feel it floating in the air.

"Just be safe, my boy." Tuno hugged him, then Emily found herself in the man's tight embrace. "I will miss you, Emily. Be safe."

Emily's throat was too clogged with tears to speak. She hugged the wonderful man back and prayed for his own safety. She couldn't even say good-bye to the little cat.

Tuno grabbed up the bed linens. "Here. I will make them into a nest for Blanche to have her kittens on, and that will explain them."

That was the last thing Emily heard from Tuno as Alex dragged her from the bedroom. Stanni was in the living room with his bundle. Alex opened the French doors to the back alley, and the siren's blaring reached an ear-deafening shriek. He peeked out and took a quick look in the alley.

"Do you think they could be trying to drive us out this way?" Emily asked.

"I thought of that," he said. "But if we stay here, we *will* be caught. This is our only chance. Stanni's coming with us so he's not caught here. He's known as a supporter of my aunt and it could cause trouble for Tuno. We'll drop him off at his house."

She nodded. Each of them flitted out into the deep night like wraiths.

Emily's heart beat in her throat as they hurried down the alley between the apartments. The air was a fresh slap in the face after being holed up inside for so long. Clouds covered the sky, hiding them in their shadows. She was fearful at what they'd left behind, and her ears strained for any other sound besides her own breath whistling in and out of her lungs. She resisted the overwhelming urge to turn around and look for pursuers. Alex's hand on her arm was tight and reassuring, like an anchor in the chaos.

She knew logically he was right about leaving Tuno and Blanche . . . and she was furious with him at the same time.

The alleyway was about one hundred yards long, and at the end they came to the garages. The street they faced was completely deserted, every house on the other side dark, as if shut off from the world. Emily silently counted off the garage doors until they came to the seventh one. Alex let go of her arm and fumbled with the lock. He cursed softly. She mentally screamed at him to hurry as she wondered if Tuno had heard that ominous knock on his door yet, and if he was safe. Finally the lock clicked audibly, and Alex swung one side open enough for them to squeeze through.

"Stanni, watch."

The younger man nodded. The garage was narrow, but they edged by the dark Mercedes. Alex unlocked the driver's door. Emily slid in past the wheel to the passenger side.

"Stanni," Alex called softly, half in and half out of the vehicle.

"Clear," Stanni said. "Start it up. I'll close the doors, and lock them after you pull out."

Alex closed the door shut and turned the key in the ignition. The car purred to life immediately. Emily sighed in relief, then went rigid. How could a normally quiet Mercedes engine suddenly sound like a roaring forty-ton diesel truck?

"They'll hear it," she whispered.

"They're too busy playing sirens."

"Alex—"

"Emily, stop being a back-seat driver."

She shut up.

Alex backed the car out quickly. Stanni swung the garage doors shut and locked them. Alex already had the car in forward and moving as Stanni opened the passenger door and slid onto the seat. Emily found herself squeezed between the two men, the submachine gun lying along her right thigh. She hadn't even noticed Stanni carrying the thing. Alex's thigh was solidly along her left.

This is not the time for this, she thought, as she felt the automatic tingle of flesh against flesh. Sitting practically on top of Alex was one way to dispel her fears. Unfortunately, it created new problems. She forced her attention to the gun pointing at her kneecap.

"Stanni," she whispered. "Would you point the muzzle away from me, please."

He moved the gun. "It's okay, Emily. There aren't any bullets."

"No bullets?" The thought was actually horrifying.

"Never have been," he said cheerfully.

"Never . . ." Then it hit her. "You scared the hell out of me that night!"

"Shh!" Alex hushed.

Emily fumed silently, not sure whether to be angry or grateful there never had been any bullets.

The car rolled down the darkened street. Alex

stopped at the corner, looked each way, then eased off the brake. They crossed the roadway and continued down the narrow street. Inside the car was silence and tension. Emily realized she was holding her breath, waiting. Waiting for the roar of another engine, a shout of alarm. She didn't let the air out of her lungs.

The car crossed another street without incidence. And another. They were on their way.

Again.

The city-limits sign on the little one-lane road was almost indiscernible in the darkness.

Alex braked and stared at it. He couldn't believe they had made it this far without incident. Well, almost without. When they'd turned onto the street Stanni lived on, they'd nearly run smack into a huge protest march against Florian. Stanni was now along for the ride. Once they got near the border, he and Emily would continue on and Stanni would take the car back to Tuno.

Still, everything had gone well—no patrols or police—although he hadn't been able to use the headlights and had had to drive at a snail's pace. His muscles were shaking with tension. They couldn't afford to get cocky, however, just because they had made it this far. They had to drive through the steep mountains above the city. The view was picturesque, and the roads treacherous.

Emily shifted in the seat. He patted her thigh in reassurance and congratulations . . . and in possessiveness. He felt that emotion flow through him and didn't know whether to curse or smile, because he couldn't stop the feeling.

Emily moved her leg, though she couldn't move

it very far. "What are you waiting for?" she asked. "The light to change?"

Stanni chuckled, and Alex grinned. "Right."

Taking his foot off the brake, he allowed the car to roll forward, gathering speed for the climb.

"Greece, here we come," Emily said.

She sounded excited. Alex couldn't blame her, but warned, "It's a long way . . . even in the best of times."

"And this is the worst." She sighed. "Thank you, Mr. Dickens. There's only one thing to do. Stanni, would you like to learn a tried-and-true American car song?"

Stanni laughed. "Of course."

In her typical tension-easing fashion, Emily began to sing. "'One hundred bottles of beer on the wall, one hundred bottles of beer . . .'"

Alex shook his head in wry amusement. Despite all his years in the States, he'd never understood that song. How could bottles of beer be on the wall? No one ever said anything about shelves, just beer on a wall. And by the time every one of them had been taken down and passed around, everybody ought to be flat on the floor, literally dead drunk. It was one of the many American contradictions that delighted him. Emily was another. In fact, she was rapidly heading to the top of the list of all things that delighted him.

He shook his head again and thought of Tuno. His stomach churned and all pleasure fled. What had happened to his friend? It didn't seem fair that they had come so far without him. Alex could feel the hard ridge of the ancient crown against his skin under his shirt. His bulky jacket hid the line of it and the other items he carried. The orb scepter sat heavily at his waist. His acute awareness had nothing to do with the feel of metal, and he wished with all his heart they weren't where they were.

In the few seconds of distraction in the bedroom, Tuno had retrieved the jewels from their hiding place and handed them to him. The moment he'd touched them, Alex had known he couldn't refuse to take them. He couldn't, even by neutrality, support his uncle. The stewardship of the House of Kiros had been placed properly with his aunt Julia.

There had been no time for anything other than to slip them under his shirt, but now he realized that next to his flesh was the safest place available. A bag could be misplaced or searched, innocently or otherwise. If they were stopped, it wouldn't matter, of course, but that was another problem.

"Emily, you're going to be drunk if you keep singing that song," Stanni said.

"No I won't," Emily said, interrupting her singing. "Didn't you notice you just pass the bottles around? Nobody ever drinks out of them."

"I've often wondered about that," Alex said, peering ahead. The road was dark and very bumpy. No headlights made it worse.

"And now you know." Her voice was tinged with amusement. "Okay, are you ready?"

"I'm not sure," Stanni muttered.

"It doesn't matter. Just start from the top anyway. 'One hundred bottles of beer on the wall—'"

The car jolted violently, the three occupants bounced out of their seats as the car slammed down and forward, coming to an instant halt.

Alex was thrown over the steering wheel. He reached out automatically and shut off the engine. Emily was piled against him, Stanni against her. They must have run off the road. His heart pounded at what he'd nearly done.

"Are you okay?" Everybody asked the same question at once.

"I guess we are," Emily gasped. "Next time remind me to use the seat belt."

"All of us." Stanni swung open his door and climbed up out of the car. Alex tried his side, but the door would only open a few inches before some obstruction stopped it.

Stanni helped Emily out, then reached in for Alex. Alex grasped his hand and scrambled up the inclined seat, Stanni pulling him along.

He stepped away from the car and immediately looked for Emily. She was hugging herself, shaken but all together. He put an arm around her and hugged her to his side. Her body seemed fragile.

"Are you sure you're okay?" he asked.

She nodded. "Nothing a good stiff drink wouldn't cure. Where's the beer when you really need it? And if I *ever* get my hands on that travel agent, I'll kill her!"

Alex chuckled. She was fine. He turned his attention to the car . . . and stared. He hadn't accidentally run off the road. He'd driven into a huge crater *in* the road. They were lucky they hadn't been killed.

"Looks like the road collapsed," Stanni said, examining the enormous hole.

"How could the road collapse?" Emily asked.

Alex shrugged. "Some of these roads are very old and not kept up as they should be."

"Or it could have had help," Stanni added. "It's better than a roadblock. You don't have to guard it, and it forces people to use the main roads. Or it could keep the soldiers from using it. Either way, it's effective."

"It certainly was effective on Tuno's car," Emily said. "Now what?"

"Got any walking songs?" Alex asked.

"Got any running songs?" Stanni pointed up the road ahead. Several pairs of headlights were swinging back and forth in a game of follow the leader as vehicles drove around the curving roadway.

"I've got a bad feeling about this," Emily said.

"So do I."

Alex no sooner pronounced the words than they were grabbing their bags and scattering into the wooded area lining the road. Tree branches whipped across their faces and bodies, sometimes slapping hard. Breathless, they struggled up behind a rock formation. Alex threw himself down on the hard ground, and Emily followed suit. The cold dirt held no comfort of sanctuary, though, and it took Alex only a few seconds to realize Stanni wasn't with them.

"Stanni?" he whispered, not daring to do more. There was no answer.

"Oh no." Emily's voice was so low, he nearly didn't catch the words.

"He's smart. He'll be fine," Alex said firmly, as much to assure himself as her.

As the clamor of several engines came closer they clung to each other. He wondered if she could feel the bulk of the jewels, but then she raised her head and he forgot everything as he gazed into her eyes.

Alex kissed her desperately, glad they were both alive. Her mouth was like soft fire as she kissed him back, licking up flames inside him. Their hands were all over each other, clinging, exploring, as the reckless desire quickened. The last thing he should be thinking about was passion, yet he could think of nothing else.

There was a loud roaring in his ears. Louder and louder. They pulled away from each other at the same moment, panting. The vehicles were directly below them on the road.

"Dorothy Sayers once called a burst of hormones 'shabby tigers,'" Emily said. "It was pretty shabby of them to show up now."

Alex grinned. "The tigers have their own minds when it comes to you."

Even as he was saying the words, he was inching forward until he could peek around the rocks. Three trucks were slowing as the Mercedes was illuminated in the first one's headlights. Alex held his breath and watched as, incredibly, the trucks veered around the car and kept going.

"What is it?" Emily asked.

"They passed by," Alex told her, in shock.

"You're kidding!" She practically crawled on top of him to peek around the rocks herself.

"You're going to raise those tigers again," he warned her.

"Sorry." She slid off him. He grunted at the sudden lifting of her weight. Not that she was heavy; she just felt damn good.

"You two make enough noise to wake the dead," Stanni said, materializing out of nowhere.

"And you could scare them awake," Alex said, climbing to his feet. He helped Emily up and did not let go of her hand. He squeezed her fingers gently, conscious of their feminine strength. "Did you see what they were?"

"It looked like farm trucks going to the city,"

Stanni answered. "Someone's determined to maintain a normal life."

"And keep the bucks coming in," Emily added. "Now what?"

"Where there are farmers," Alex said, "there's bound to be a village. Maybe we can get help with the car."

"I don't think it's going anywhere if we do," Stanni said. "The front end was smashed."

Alex groaned. "Tuno's going to kill me. Emily, I do believe we've just received our walking papers."

"The thrill of a lifetime."

Stanni handed over the bag of food to Alex, and Emily's flight bag to her. "Look, why don't I take care of the car and get it back to Tuno? That would help cover the two of you."

"Stanni," Alex began, despite the younger man's logic. The thought of leaving him was repugnant.

"You better get moving." Stanni clapped him on the shoulder. "Next time it may not be farmers heading to market."

"I really am going to kill my travel agent," Emily said. "And don't laugh."

Alex laughed anyway. He wanted to keep on laughing with her, but first he had to get them out of this.

Greece was a long way away.

Six

"'Valderie-e-e, valdera-a-a, valdera-a-a, valde-ha-ha-ha . . .'"

Emily groaned as she listened to Alex sing the official walking song of every hiking organization known to mankind.

"How long will it take us to walk to Greece?" she asked, trudging along next to him and shading her eyes from the bright afternoon sun. She was hot and tired and thirsty, and he'd been singing that song for the last half hour.

"About a week," Alex said, interrupting himself.

"A week!" She gaped at him. "I hope you know more songs than that one."

He frowned. "What's wrong with this one?"

"Nothing, except that I'll really need the 'bones in the basket' phrase if you sing it for an entire week. Could we stop now? We've been walking since we left Stanni, and that was before dawn. Besides, I'm tired of trees slapping me in the face. It makes me feel like a degenerate."

"Good idea." He gave her a mock leer. "I could be the degenerate instead."

"Let's keep moving," she said, speeding up despite her sore feet.

"And miss all this wonderful sunshine? Emily, you strike me as a woman who would stop and smell the roses in the middle of a revolution."

"I'm smelling, Alex. Trust me."

Keep the relationship light, she sternly reminded herself. That meant no flirting. No touching. Even no looking. Events had happened so fast since last night, she'd been caught up in them without thought. Now, alone with him as they made their way alongside the road, always keeping to the protective bushes and trees, she was beginning to realize she was *alone* with him. Alone with a sexy prince. Already she was constantly aware of his body's movement, the stretch of those long legs, the easy swing of his strong arms. The air was filled with the scent of the pine woods they were hiking through, but her imagination conjured up the scent of him when he'd kissed her that morning. That kiss, a desperate need for each other in the midst of danger, had touched off a fierce, primitive craving in her. He really wasn't a handsome man, not classically handsome, but he exuded virility. The sexuality was a presence, a cloak mantling the man, enticing her with what was below the surface. She couldn't trust herself with him.

"Oh, brother," she muttered. She was worse off than she'd thought. Her dire situation was all she ought to be concerned with, and instead it took a back seat to this man. She could no sooner stop her imagination from creating erotic fantasies about him, than she could stop her heart from beating wildly every time he touched her. This Stockholm Syndrome was getting way out of hand. And that's all it was, she insisted to herself.

"Emily," he said, jolting her from her disturbing thought, "don't worry about Tuno and Blanche. They're all right."

She glanced at him. "Do you really believe that?"

"I have to. We're not there, so that makes him safe, right?"

"I suppose."

"And I'm sure Blanche had her kittens with no problem."

She nodded. Weariness caught up with her, and suddenly she felt exhausted.

"Come on." He took her arm and pulled her deeper into the woods, away from the road. "Let's take a break and have something to eat. We've been pushing ourselves for too long."

The odd pounding in her veins that started when he began to lead her to a more secluded area, faded at his words. They were just going to eat lunch, she told herself. What had she expected? She decided not to answer that question. She really didn't want to know.

The woods became more lush with undergrowth and the ground sloped sharply upward. Emily panted as they climbed up the steep grade. The trees were thicker and more primordial. She was breathless when they finally stopped in a shaded glen.

"What are you?" she asked, flopping down on a flat-topped boulder. "A wayward member of the Von Trapp family?"

"You need more exercise, Emily," he said, drawing in a deep breath. "Good, fresh mountain air. What more could a person ask for?"

"A limo and a passport?"

He laughed. "And a jug of wine and thou."

"'Thou' had better not be drinking wine while driving," she said, wondering how he could be so damn cheerful when their little world was collapsing.

"'Thou' has only water." He pulled a bottle from the bag. "If a limo should drop from the sky, we're safe enough. I think."

She realized he was deliberately maintaining a jaunty air to keep her calm . . . to keep her from worrying . . . to make her feel safe and relaxed. She turned away, more touched by the gesture than she cared to admit.

"We've got salami and cheese and apples," he said.

"And I've got the breath mints," she said, rummaging through her flight bag. She could reciprocate the mood, for his sake.

"We're set. So tell me about growing up on a horse farm in Pennsylvania. At least, I presume that's where your family's farm was, since you said you teach school in that state."

"My family's home is there," she said. "West Chester County. Horse country. There isn't much to tell, really. It's a mix of suburbia and rural life. About the only major event throughout my childhood was my five older brothers torturing me on a regular basis. I grew up to like them anyway."

He chuckled, slicing off a hunk of cheese from the small brick. "I expect you were a tomboy through and through."

"Hard not to be under the circumstances," she said, taking the cheese from him. "Cut two of the salami so I can make a sort of sandwich with them."

He nodded, following her directions. After handing the salami over, he asked, "So how's your love life, Emily Cooper?"

She nearly dropped the food. "Ahh . . ."

"Do you have any boyfriends? You don't wear a ring, so I assume there's no husband. Am I wrong? You said before there was no man. How much does no man mean no man? Was there ever a husband?"

"There was one once," she said reluctantly. "Now there's not."

"What happened?"

She nibbled on her "sandwich."

"Emily."

"He married me on the rebound from a broken engagement." Her voice was uncharacteristically sharp, for she felt vulnerable about her past.

"I see."

She had a sense he saw more than she liked.

"So what happened?" he asked.

She shrugged. "The usual."

"What's the usual? Fighting over money? Lifestyle differences? He got offered a job across the country and you didn't want to go? Adultery?"

"No!" She drew in a calming breath. "Lifestyle differences."

"How different? He wanted the towels folded in thirds and you didn't?"

She groaned, feeling the trap of non-answers. By telling him more about herself, she was letting him through intimate doors. But by not telling him, she was acknowledging she was afraid to allow him inside.

She decided telling was safer in several ways. At least she could control what she told him. "I was a senior in college and my roommate dumped her fiancé. I gave Hank tea and sympathy because I liked him. Somehow we wound up married, and even now I still can't figure out how it happened. My mother says I'm the eternal maternal. Anyway, we both realized it was a mistake, so we ended it." She decided not to tell him about her broken engagement, which had been a near mirror of her marriage until she came to her senses. Neither did she want to tell him that that was the reason she'd come to Peraco, to get away from everything. Instead she went on the attack. "So what about you? Any marriages or great loves lurking in your past?"

"I had this wild crush on Peggy Lipton of the "Mod Squad" when I was a kid, and one marriage now kaput. And before you ask, she was disappointed she married a plain vanilla instead of a prince."

"How did you become a plain vanilla anyway?" she asked, beginning to feel relaxed and at ease. The breeze wafting through the glen cooled her skin. The rock felt comfortably hard against her back. The cheese and salami weren't bad, either.

He shrugged. "After all my family's antics, I'm grateful to be a plain vanilla."

"What antics?"

"Collecting clocks that don't work, breaking out in hives when faced with business decisions, sponsoring a charity for cockroaches, and locking young cousins in the palace cellar. It's dark and scary down there." He laughed at himself. "Eight hundred years of inbreeding catches up with itself in odd ways, so good old plain vanilla has a lot of appeal."

She bet it did. From what he'd told her and from what she'd seen, his family was definitely left of center. She realized he worked hard at being plain

The Publisher
of Loveswept®
Romances
invites you to:

CLAIM
A FREE
EXCLUSIVE
ROMANCE

Lift Here

...PLUS SIX
ROMANCES
RISK FREE

NO
OBLIGATION
TO BUY!

THE FREE
GIFT IS YOURS
TO KEEP

Detach and affix this stamp to
the postage-paid reply card
and mail at once!

SEE DETAILS INSIDE ▶

LET YOURSELF BE LOVESWEPT BY... SIX BRAND NEW LOVESWEPT ROMANCES!

Because Loveswept romances sell themselves ... we want to send you six (Yes, six!) exciting new novels to enjoy for 15 days — risk free! — without obligation to buy.

Discover how these compelling stories of contemporary romances tug at your heart strings and keep you turning the pages. Meet true-to-life characters you'll fall in love with as their romances blossom. Experience their challenges and triumphs — their laughter, tears and passion.

Let yourself be Loveswept! Join our **at-home reader service!** Each month we'll send you six new Loveswept novels **before they appear in the bookstores.** Take up to **15 days to preview** current selections **risk-free! Keep only those shipments you want.** Each book is yours for only $2.25 plus postage & handling, and sales tax in N.Y. — **a savings of 50¢ per book** off the cover price.

NO OBLIGATION TO BUY — WITH THIS RISK-FREE OFFER!

YOU GET SIX
ROMANCES RISK FREE...
Plus AN EXCLUSIVE TITLE FREE!

Loveswept Romances

Kay Hooper's
Larger Than Life

This FREE gift
is yours to keep.

MY "NO RISK" GUARANTEE

There's no obligation to buy and the free gift is mine to keep. I may preview each
subsequent shipment for 15 days. If I don't want it, I simply return the books
within 15 days and owe nothing. If I keep them, I will pay just $2.25 per book. I
save $3.00 off the retail price for the 6 books (plus postage and handling, and
sales tax in NY).

YES! Please send my six Loveswept novels
RISK FREE along with my FREE GIFT
described inside the heart! **BR90** 41228

NAME_____

ADDRESS_____ APT_____

CITY_____

STATE_____ ZIP_____

vanilla to ensure he wasn't like them. Sympathy welled up inside her for the little boy locked in the palace cellar. It must have been horrifying . . .

Instantly she stamped out the urge to comfort. It had gotten her into trouble before.

"What's it like teaching five-year-olds?" he asked. "You said your students were unpredictable."

This was safer ground. "It's a lot like *Kindergarten Cop*. A teacher has to be half actress to keep them entertained and half policeman to keep them from chaos."

"They should have hired you at the palace. Our tutors had about as much effect as mushrooms with my cousins."

"Maybe they were afraid to discipline royalty."

"You wouldn't have been."

She grinned. "Probably not. They're just kids who need guidance. Children thrive on routine and common sense discipline."

He nodded and ate silently, as if contemplating her words. She finished her own meal, deciding the lack of conversation was better than the direction it had been going in. She didn't want to know more about him. The more she knew, the more curious she became, and it would spiral around and around until she was truly caught in its web. She only wanted to get home to her class and her life. Plain old everyday vanilla.

So why did plain vanilla have all the appeal of a match striking into a blaze?

"How're your feet?" Alex asked.

"Fine," she lied. There was a constant ache along her soles, and she was all too aware of every bone in her foot, signals that her feet were in trouble. She looked at his expensive loafers, now scuffed beyond salvation. His feet had to be worse. "How're yours?"

"Wishing we had the car." He stood up and grimaced. "Or a wheelchair. Think you could push me all the way to Greece?"

"How far is 'all the way'?"

"Well, we've come about ten miles—"

"Ten!" she exclaimed. "That's all? Ten?"

"How far did you think we'd come?"

"I don't know. It seemed like forever."

"It will be, at the rate we're going."

She sighed, depressed at the thought.

He held out his hand to her. "Come on, Emily. We won't get there by sitting around feeling sorry for ourselves."

Reluctantly she took his hand, and he helped her to her feet. Her senses sizzled at the strength and warmth of his fingers wrapped around hers. She stared up at him, unable to find the willpower to look away.

"Emily." His voice was husky.

His head lowered. His lips touched hers tentatively, as if he were uncertain about her reaction. He caressed her mouth so gently, she thought her heart would break. The pressure was like warm silk, wrapping her in a dark, delicate cocoon. He didn't touch her any further, didn't pull her to him with a burst of passion. Instead, the reined-in desire had its own magic. It was a seduction of tenderness she couldn't fight. She didn't even try.

Finally he lifted his head. "We better get moving."

She nodded, not daring to suggest they rest more. The glen was too inviting, and it was clear how they would eventually forget their troubles. It was as if all their attraction had been released since leaving Tuno's.

Neither apologized for shabby tigers. They had been elegant this time.

And all the more frightening.

"Are you kidding?" Emily asked.

"Do you have any better suggestions?" Alex countered, staring at the barn looming in the dusk.

"Yes. The ground, with two nice hard rocks for pillows. I don't want to sleep in a barn, Alex. The farmer could come in and catch us. Then where would we be?"

A farmer was the least of his worries, Alex thought. This afternoon had proven more dangerous to his equilibrium than he'd imagined. All day that wondrous kiss had floated through his mind. Somehow it had kept him going, sore feet and all. But he could barely walk now, his handmade loafers a joke. And Emily was beyond exhausted. They had pushed themselves too hard. They needed rest and comfort, and the ground and rocks couldn't begin to provide that. He'd just keep his distance from her, that's all.

"We're sleeping in the barn," he said, moving forward. She squawked in protest, and he scowled at her. "Shh! You'll bring the farmer down on us for sure."

"You're crazy," she whispered, walking up next to him.

"Do you have hay fever?"

"No."

"Then I'm not crazy."

He skirted the edge of the woods, watching the

lighted farmhouse. It looked like the occupants were in for the night.

"What time do cows have to be milked?" he asked.

"How should I know? I was raised on a horse farm, remember?"

"Right." Without warning, he grabbed her hand and plunged across the open space between trees and building. They covered the ground in seconds, then flattened themselves against the barn wall. The rough wood dug into his back.

"I wonder if James Bond does this stuff," Emily said.

"Hush up, woman. I'm trying to find you a bed for the night and you're yakking away about it."

He guided her around the barn, away from the lights of the house, looking for a window or side door.

"Where are the damn doors?" he muttered, feeling for any break in the wall.

"Back where we came from," Emily whispered. "Didn't you see them?"

"No, I didn't see them," he replied, feeling stupid as she led the way back.

The swing doors were seamed into the wood walls and padlocked with one small metal latch and lock, not barred with the huge four-by-eight length of wood he'd been looking for. Barn doors always had that in the movies. Emily touched a piece of wood and a smaller door built into the large one swung inward. She vanished within.

"Emily!" He stepped over the door ledge and into the dark barn.

"Right here." She swung the door shut, closing off the last of the light. Cracks between the wood allowed only dim slivers in now.

The odor of animal and hay overwhelmed his senses. Horses nickered and shuffled in their stalls. A cow lowed.

"I hope she's been milked," he said, taking Emily's hand again. "Think there's an empty stall we can sleep in?"

"This is your little foray." He knew she was grinning at him. "However, a good farmer checks his stock one last time before going to bed, so if I may suggest the hay loft above . . ."

"Lead on."

They found the ladder and clamored up the rungs into the loft. The noises and smells were fainter up there, and the animals were settling down, unconcerned with the newcomers. Alex immediately relaxed.

"Looks better than the Hilton," he said, making out the piles of hay strewn around the large area. "As long as the house detective doesn't knock on the door, we'll be okay."

"You hope." Her voice was dubious. She sank down into some hay. "I'm scared to take off my shoes. My feet will probably balloon up into basketballs."

Alex found her in the darkness and settled on the hay slightly away from her. Something told him to keep space between them.

"I have a feeling mine are going to be bigger than basketballs," he said.

"I have a foot bath at home," she said wistfully. "The nice warm water swirls around—"

"Please, no water torture." He drew in a deep breath, then popped his shoes off. "What does it mean when there's no change in the level of agony?"

"That your feet fell off five miles back."

"That explains it."

"How far do you think we've come today?"

He paused, as if calculating. He didn't want to disappoint her, but their route had been more circuitous than direct, in order to avoid the larger towns and villages. "We've put a fair distance between us and the car. Probably about twenty miles."

"Oh." She was obviously disappointed.

He passed food and the water bottle to her, rather than try to find a placating conversation. Sometimes it was better to leave things be, he decided. Besides, he couldn't lie to her about how long their journey would take. Emily deserved better than lies . . . about anything.

Dinner was the same as lunch, and they ate in silence, listening to the animals below and the natural noises of the woods outside. An owl hooted from somewhere near. By the time he finished eating, Alex was completely relaxed—except for his feet. Hers had to be as bad. They'd both be crippled if they didn't do something. Her words about a foot bath came back. He couldn't provide that, but he could provide another method of relaxation.

"Here." He lifted her right foot onto his lap and began to massage it.

"What do you think you're doing?" she asked, trying to yank her foot out of his grasp.

He held it firmly. "Insuring you can walk tomorrow. If I don't do this, you won't even be able to stand in the morning." He plopped his foot onto her thigh with all the finesse of a toddler. "Do mine. *Please*. I'd just like to know they're still there."

Clinically, he kneaded her flesh, ignoring her hesitancy. Her muscles were so cramped and stiff, they felt like rocks. He wished they did have a foot bath, one of those little Jacuzzi-type things. They couldn't continue at the pace he'd set for them that day. They weren't properly dressed, nor did they have the equipment for hiking across mountainous terrain. He blamed himself for the car, knowing he'd been too paranoid. He could have used the headlights judiciously. He'd have to do something to rectify this little problem if they were to get to Greece. Maybe the farmer had a pair of old sneakers in the right size that he could pinch.

Emily began to rub his foot weakly, then more forcefully, digging into his muscles almost painfully. It felt good. So good, in fact, he reconsidered stealing a pair of better shoes. It would be nice to have Emily rub his feet each night.

As the silence grew into long minutes, he slowly became aware of the way the heel of Emily's foot was resting against his pelvis. Every time he stretched her foot, her heel sank farther against him in a countermovement. Right against him. Little beads of sweat popped out on his forehead. He wondered if this was how foot fetishists got started. A little innocent foot in the lap and one went kinky for life.

"Ouch!" she exclaimed. "You're yanking on it."

He relaxed his grip. "Sorry. This foot's probably done anyway."

"I'll say."

He patted her foot and set it aside, then took up the other one, this time setting it well down on his thigh. He concentrated on manipulating the flesh to loosen the muscles and unstiffen the joints, priding himself on keeping the task a task . . . until he became aware of his foot wedged between her thighs. They were enticingly soft, the underlying muscles firm. He wondered how they would feel wrapped around his waist, holding him tightly as he moved inside her . . .

Sweat trickled down his temples, and he cursed under his breath. He wanted to pull his foot away, but he couldn't move. He could only feel those small feminine hands creating a sensual voodoo that stole his control.

When she finally set his foot aside, he was breathless. Released from her magic, he pushed her foot off his leg as if it were a burning brand.

He couldn't explain his reaction. Ten minutes earlier he had been ready to collapse in agony and exhaustion, and now he was pent-up, restless . . .

His brain nudged him about something he needed to tell her. The jewels. That would distract him. Throughout their trek, he'd considered whether or not to tell her. She really ought to know what he'd gotten them into.

"Emily," he whispered.

"What?" Her voice floated back to him, low and sensual.

He forced himself not to respond to that ripple of dark silk across his skin. "There's something you should know. I have the crown jewels."

She gasped. "The *what* jewels?"

"The crown jewels of Peraco," he said quickly, realizing she thought he meant something cruder.

"You mean what a king would wear?"

"Yes. Tuno gave them to me last night, to take them out of the country and prevent the coronation. I thought you should know."

"Oh, Lordy." He could hear the excitement in her voice. "Really, Alex? Where are they? Can I see them?"

"How? There's almost no light." He wondered if he'd made a mistake. She sounded almost gleeful.

"Yes there is." He heard the zipper of her flight bag being dragged open. "I've got a flashlight on my key chain."

With a snap, a tiny beam of light played across the hay, then straight into his eyes. He squinted.

"Where are they?"

"Here. And point that thing away from me." He unbuttoned his shirt and pulled out the velvet pouch, laying it on the hay. He pushed open the mouth of the bag and took out the jewels. There was a long silence as she examined them.

"You're kidding," she said, sounding disappointed.

"They're over a thousand years old," he said, annoyed at her reaction. Didn't she understand the *history* involved? "They didn't go in for fancy in those days."

"Really? A thousand years." She reached out and touched the pendant. "Incredible."

"Thank you for being properly awed." He paused. "I'm sorry I got you mixed up in this part. But I couldn't refuse them."

"Oh, Alex. I think you're wonderful."

"You do?" The notion pleased the hell out of him.

"Yes, I do. You're saving your family's country. I'm—I'm proud to know you . . . to have been a part of this." She snapped off the flashlight. "Well, we've got to get out of Peraco now. Here, let's put them into the flight bag."

"I'll carry it." He closed the pouch and put it in the flight bag. They sat quietly for a few minutes. "Emily."

"What?"

"Nothing."

"Oh."

He leaned forward, telling himself not to be a fool as he did. His hand touched hers.

Emily swallowed as a sensual lightning bolt jolted through her. "I hope that's you."

"It is." She was so close. He shouldn't be courting emotional danger like this, but he couldn't stop himself.

"You're not . . ." She cleared her throat. "You're not going to kiss me or anything, are you?"

He leaned forward even more, until he could feel her breath on his face. "I don't think so."

"Good . . . good . . . It wouldn't be a smart idea." She didn't pull away.

"Not smart," he agreed.

His mouth found hers in the smartest move he'd ever made. Her lips were warm, opening under his the way a flower opens under the sun. He pressed her back into the hay, settling his body on her, feeling her breasts against his chest. Her tongue twined with his, teasing and tormenting, driving his blood hotter and hotter. He hungered for her, like a man too long deprived of nourishment.

Emily dug her fingers into his shoulders, not caring what the consequences would be. She wanted him. He'd overwhelmed her senses, overwhelmed her cautions, overwhelmed her. How could she fight him, especially when he finally showed he trusted her? Her swiftly building passion washed away her weariness. From the beginning, she'd wanted him. Each day they had together was a gift, and she would squander no gift.

His mouth was a fire, burning her up. His hands

dragged across her breasts, pushing her out of control. She lifted herself into him, straining for a deeper touch. He rained kisses on her cheeks, her throat. His hands practically ripped the sweater and shirt from her. The hay was scratchy beneath her, but the moment her breasts were free and his lips found one nipple, she forgot everything in the sensual onslaught. His teeth nipped gently and his tongue laved her, until she was writhing beneath him, his touch driving her need beyond sanity. She heard herself moan his name and she didn't care. Her fingers somehow got his shirt off, and she moaned again at the feel of his flesh against her flesh, hot skin against hot skin. His body shifted over hers, the denim of their jeans rasping together. Her legs opened to cradle his hips. She bent her knee to caress his calf with her foot—

And shrieked as intense pain gripped her leg in a charley horse the size of Saint Louis.

"What? What?" Alex demanded, jumping off her. He yelped and grabbed his own leg as his muscles suddenly knotted.

"Charley horse!" she gasped, curling into a ball. Tears rolled down her face, pooling at her mouth. She could taste the salt on her lips. She should have known this would happen after all that walking.

"Stretch your leg out . . ." His voice held great pain. "Keep the foot flat . . . ahhh . . . don't point . . . toe!"

"I know." She tried to follow his advice, but her leg protested violently.

"Too much walk . . ." He groaned as muscles clearly knotted in a new spot.

Too much something, she thought. Whimpering, she tried to stretch her leg again, gritting her teeth against the cramp. The pain was still tremendous, but it felt better somehow.

Embarrassment heated her face as she realized she was nude from the waist up. She felt around for her shirt or sweater, and her fingers finally touched cotton. She pulled the shirt around her before noticing it was Alex's shirt, not hers. She flung it away, then grabbed her leg again as a new pain hit.

"This is ridiculous," she muttered, cursing her luck. But it figured. There must be a sign across her forehead that said "sucker." When her leg calmed enough, she went on the great shirt hunt again, this time with more success.

"Are you okay?" Alex asked.

"Yes. I hope we didn't rouse the farmer."

"We'll know in a few minutes."

They waited in tense silence. Emily spent the time berating herself for giving in to the moment. The leg cramp had been a punishment for her foolishness, she decided. She had allowed herself to think that she could make love with Alex and then walk away without an emotional scratch. Well, her body had saved her from pain and humiliation, and she ought to be grateful.

When no maddened farmer showed up, they eventually relaxed into awkward silence. Determined to dispel it, Emily sat up and gathered the flight bag to her. "I get charley horses sometimes and I brought something with me from home. I hope the cramping doesn't go on all night, but just in case . . ."

She rummaged around and pulled out a small bottle. "Here we go. It's just an over-the-counter muscle relaxant, but it's effective enough."

"Maybe we'll be able to hobble tomorrow," he said, straightening up. "I'll get some water."

They took the pills, then gingerly settled back in the hay.

"I think I'll go to sleep now," she said, curling up several feet away from him. She kept her back to him.

"Good night, Emily," he said. From the direction of his voice, she could tell he was lying on his back.

"Good night, Alex." Then, not able to resist, she added, "Good night, John Boy. Good night, Pa. Good night, Ma. Good night, Grandpa. Good night, Grandma—"

"Say good night, Gracie."

"Good night, Gracie."

The playfulness took the tension out of her. And out of him, too, she thought, sensing an easing in him. But he would have to find different accommodations than these from now on. She didn't trust herself in ones as comfortable as this.

Seven

After a dead sleep, Alex awoke bleary-eyed to daylight and Emily snuggled against his side. How she came there he didn't ask. He didn't have time.

An angry farmer was glaring down at him, holding a pitchfork to his belly.

Alex had a feeling today wouldn't go quite as well as yesterday.

"What the hell are you doing in my barn?" the farmer asked in Peracan.

"Sleeping." Alex watched the razor-sharp tines cautiously. He wanted to reach out and touch the flight bag with its priceless contents, but he didn't dare move. He didn't think the farmer would hurt him or Emily, but he really didn't want to find out.

"I can see that you're sleeping," the farmer said. He pulled the pitchfork back slightly, but still kept it at the ready. "You don't look like tramps. Are you coming from the troubles of the city?"

Alex nodded. "We're Greeks heading home."

"And I'm the King of Sheba." The farmer's switch from perfectly accented Peracan to perfectly accented English was so swift, Alex could only blink at the change. Clearly, the man was a transplanted Brit. "You're dressed too well and too American to be a nice Greek fellow heading home with his wife. Besides, that's not a Greek accent you're sporting, mate. I've lived here too long not to know the difference."

Alex realized his well-laid plans had been blown to hell with one slip of the tongue. His stomach tensed at the thought that this man might recognize him . . . if he hadn't already.

Emily stirred against his side.

"Emily," he said gently, laying his arm across her so she wouldn't jump up in fright and scare their antagonist into using the pitchfork. "It's our wake-up call."

"Wake-up call?" She pried her eyes open and stared at him. He waited for awareness to kick in. When it did, her eyes widened only slightly as she looked past him to the farmer.

"Good morning," she said cheerfully, though her body tensed. "Sorry about borrowing your hay. We'll gladly put it back in nice pile order."

"She's not even bloody Greek!" the farmer exclaimed. "What the hell is going on here?"

Emily muttered a barnyard curse under her breath.

"That's about what we're in," Alex murmured to her, cautiously letting her go. "Look, we're tourists who can't get to the embassy to get home, so we're trying to reach the border. We're sorry we gave you a fright, but we'll just move on, okay?"

"I don't know." The farmer's suspicions were obviously escalating. "We're supposed to help any strangers *to* the local police station. What for, I can't figure out. Better come up to the house and get a decent meal from the wife while I decide what to do with you. Damn, but I don't need this headache today."

The pitchfork went upright. Alex slowly got to his feet. Pain shot through him, and he was all too aware of a lingering tenderness in his calf from the charley horse. He helped Emily up. She had the presence of mind to pick up the flight bag casually, setting the strap over her head so it wound diagonally across her body. It would be almost impossible to snatch it from her without a fight. He grabbed their shoes, then they slowly made their way to the ladder. His heart dropped as he realized she wasn't faking her pain any more than he was. They certainly couldn't make a run for it in their condition.

"You still haven't answered my question about who you are," the farmer said.

"Al and Emily Cooper," Alex said smoothly, pleased his brain was in good working order. Emily blinked, but didn't contradict him.

"Jimmy Waites. You two walk from Seriat?" the farmer asked. "In those shoes?"

They nodded.

"I'm surprised you're even upright today."

"Me too," Alex muttered, wincing as he set his feet on the hard wooden rungs of the ladder. Unfortunately, the thought of putting his feet into his shoes brought even worse horrors to the mind.

"Your mare's down," Emily said, when she reached the floor of the barn. She peered into one of the stalls.

"She's in labor, and in trouble, too, I think," Jimmy said. "That's why I don't need the headache of you two today."

Before Alex could stop her, she stepped into the

stall. "Breech? I was raised on a horse farm . . . No, look, the foal's hooves are sticking out."

"And that's it," Jimmy said, going in after her. "I've been here over an hour and she's made no progress. I can't feel the foal's head in the canal."

Alex followed behind the farmer, staring at the mare, whose burgeoning sides were heaving in her distress.

"I'll bet its head is turned back," Emily said. "Have you called your vet?"

"Yes, but he's at another farm with another delivery." He added glumly, "By the time he gets here, it could be too late."

"If you could get a rope around the foal's head or even its nose or bottom jaw, you could pull it forward maybe. My dad did it once, applying steady counterpressure between contractions." She turned to the big Englishman, worry creasing her brow. "If you don't do something, you'll lose them both."

He stared at her for a long tense minute, obviously weighing whether she knew what she was talking about. "Right," he said abruptly.

Alex watched in amazement as Emily and the farmer went to work. Emily talked to the mare the entire time in a soothing tone, every ounce of her emotional strength bent on helping the horse through her difficult labor. "The eternal maternal" she said her mother called her, and the woman had been right. Wisely staying out of the way, he watched Emily fight for a foal's life. Possessiveness was a weak term for what he felt for her. She was gentle and beautiful and sexy. It figured she would appear in his life the moment it was turned upside down. She would never be boring. She didn't know how.

He could have escaped ten times over and the farmer never would have noticed, but of course he stayed. He wouldn't leave Emily. Somehow they got the rope around the foal's lip. Emily kept it taut, for they'd decided she didn't have the strength to do the foal further damage by tugging too hard. Neither held out much hope for the foal's survival, though. Tears trickled down Emily's face as the foal's legs would appear, only to disappear again. Alex wished he could comfort her, her pained expression touching his heart, but there was nothing he could do.

After over an hour, Emily suddenly gasped and let go of the rope. "He's come around! Just all of a sudden and pop! I could feel the head swing forward. Look! Look!"

The foal's nose peeked out of the birth canal. Jimmy grabbed its legs and pulled. With a heave on the mare's part, the foal shot forward onto the straw. It lay there unmoving.

Emily grabbed up a handful of straw and began to rub the little animal briskly. "Come on, baby, breathe for Aunt Emily."

With a shudder, it finally did. Everyone released a huge sigh of relief, and the farmer pushed the foal to the mare's nose. She looked at the shivering lump as if to say, "So that was the holdup," then nuzzled her baby. Alex decided he'd never felt so good in his life.

"Makes up for Blanche," Emily said, looking at him.

He grinned down at her over the edge of the stall. "Makes up for a lot. You were sensational."

"Not too shabby. I'm just glad it worked." She pushed herself to her feet.

The farmer righted her when she staggered on

sore muscles. "Come on, let's have some break-
fast. Then we'll put you two in a proper bed.
Neither of you is walking anywhere today."

Alex smiled. Jimmy wasn't about to turn them
in after Emily's help. The eternal maternal had
struck again.

Right when they needed it the most.

Emily stared at the double bed. The narrow,
barely-able-to-hold-one-person-let-alone-two double bed.

"Ahhh . . ." she began, her brain scrambling to
find some way to ask Jimmy's wife, Helena, for a
different room. It wouldn't be easy with "Al Cooper" attached to her hip, though. At least he
hadn't taken a bath with her earlier. Now she was
dressed in Helena's bathrobe, the woman determined to clean her clothes. Her sore muscles,
worse after helping the mare, wouldn't last long in
their current relaxed state if she didn't lie down
and rest. But not in *that* bed.

"This looks wonderful," "Al" said. She could see
him smothering a grin.

"There are towels in the bathroom for you,"
Helena said to Alex, pushing the curtains closed
against the early afternoon sun. She had fed them
an enormous lunch, not even blinking at the
sudden appearance of guests. "Feel free to rest
here until dinner. You both look exhausted."

Helena slipped from the room.

"Nice people," Alex said. "And interesting. Anybody who settles here in Peraco just to protest
England's Inland Revenue Tax has to be."

"They've got a nice farm," Emily said absently,
her attention focused on the room Jimmy and

Helena had offered, insisting they spend the night.

She didn't feel tired, not with anxiety sweeping through her. She had been saved by a couple of knotted muscles last night, but today common sense had finally kicked in. "Alex, I'm not going to sleep in that bed with you."

"Helena will think it very strange," he said, raising his eyebrows. "So will Jimmy. He's promised us a ride almost to the border in the morning. We can't afford to arouse suspicion—"

"Oh no you don't." She put her hands on her hips. "You're not going to use that on me. I'll sleep on the floor—"

"Oh no you won't. If anybody sleeps on the floor, it's me."

"Okay." She grinned at his shocked expression. "You're a prince of a guy, Alex."

"I'm an idiot," he muttered.

She sat down on the bed, then lifted her legs onto the nice soft mattress. Her body sank slightly, and she felt as if she were lying on a cloud. She sighed at the pleasure of it.

"Better than sex?" he asked, staring down at her.

She cleared her throat in a precursor to clearing the air. "About last night . . . It was just hormones—"

"So you've said before."

"Well, what else could it be? We have nothing in common."

"That's half the fun."

"Alex, I am not interested in a vacation fling, okay?"

"Okay." Suddenly he was sounding like her, agreeing too quickly and pulling a trick. But she couldn't see what the trick was. That made her even more nervous.

He bent down and patted her cheek. "Don't worry so much, Emily. I think I'll go take a bath. Why don't you nap?"

He strolled out of the room, closing the door after him. Emily stared at the ceiling. This husband-and-wife business was rapidly getting out of hand. She had to make it clear that while she might physically respond to him, she wasn't interested in a fling. And it was ludicrous even to think about anything else. The problem was, she was enamored of him being a prince. One mention of a title and she was falling all over him, probably like every other woman he knew. She had to stop thinking with tea and sympathy.

She wished she could ask for a different room, but she knew he was right about arousing suspicions. Jimmy was grateful for their help that morning, but she had no doubt the moment they did something out of the ordinary, he'd be hauling them down to the police station. And then the fireworks would really start.

She just had to get through an afternoon and a night in this room with Alex. She could at least do that, to help him get out of the country with the coronation jewels. He was so brave, so . . .

Emily realized she was doing it again, dredging up tea and sympathy. She pulled one of the pillows out from under the worn chenille bedspread and tossed it onto the floor.

"Your bed's made," she muttered.

With that, she rolled over, closed her eyes, and promptly fell asleep.

"Very funny," Alex murmured a half hour later, staring at the pillow on the throw rug. The flight bag was next to the night stand, right where it had been when he'd left the room. At least Helena hadn't taken it. He'd been worried when she'd taken his dirty clothes out of the bathroom, insistent on cleaning them, while he'd been in the tub. She'd left him a shirt and a pair of Jimmy's jeans.

A glance at Emily told him she'd been hit with a sledgehammer by Mr. Sandman. She was lying on her side, her mouth slack and open. A faint, unladylike snort reached his ears. Yep, she was out.

He stretched, marveling at the freeness of his muscles since the bath. He'd even borrowed Jimmy's razor, hoping he wouldn't mind. What was a razor among friends, anyway?

Alex wondered about that, then eyed the bed. Really, he couldn't allow Emily to establish a precedent. It was bad for the husband-and-wife image. Besides, he'd be damned if he'd sleep on a hard, uninviting wooden floor.

He picked up the pillow and set it back in its rightful place, but on top of the bedspread. Lying down, he was careful not to disturb the sleeping beauty. She didn't move, and he couldn't help grinning. She was something. Really something. He had to agree with her that a vacation fling held no interest. Something had happened to him that morning as he'd watched her perform a miracle. She had changed, become clearer in his mind . . . and his heart.

He was beginning to want a long, slow romance with her. He could feel her warmth across the few inches that separated them. It tempted him, but now that he knew what he wanted, the temptation was easier to resist. He could wait, and in the meantime he'd be the absolute gentleman a prince ought to be.

It would be interesting to see what Emily thought of that.

Emily opened her eyes as she drifted into wake-fulness. She stared at the broad male back pressed against her nose. The *naked* broad male back.

She scooted off the bed and sighed in relief as her broader view revealed that Alex still wore his pants.

"Hey!" she said, gingerly shaking his shoulder. The feel of his warm skin was enough to make her want to jump back into bed with him. "Get up!"

He rolled over on his back and opened one eye. "Hello there."

"What the hell are you doing in my bed?" she demanded, trying to keep from staring at the soft dark hair on his chest that tapered down in a thin line to his waist.

"Sleeping."

A knock sounded at the door. "Emily, Al," Helena called. "Are you awake?"

"Yes!" Emily answered.

"Good. Dinner will be shortly. You shouldn't sleep too long or you'll get your clocks mixed up."

"Thanks." She swung back to Alex. "Dinner-time."

He stretched his arms over his head. Every muscle in his chest and stomach rippled under his tanned skin. The breath rushed out of her body as if she'd just stepped into a vacuum. She tried to drag air back into her lungs, but there was none to be had in the room.

"I feel one hundred percent better." He rose from the bed and put on his borrowed shirt. The vacuum disappeared and air rushed back into her lungs. He turned around to face her. "Let's go down, shall we?"

She nodded, not trusting her voice. She knew it would come out all hoarse and needy, betraying her.

Emily marshaled all her willpower and self-control throughout dinner and the rest of the evening. When they finally retired to the bedroom, she felt ready to handle the temptation. As Alex closed the door, she picked up her pillow and settled on the floor. "I'll sleep here."

"Afraid, Emily?" he taunted.

Yes, her brain screamed. "It's my turn."

"No it's not."

He hauled her up in his arms. She squawked and fought him, sliding down and out from under him. He grabbed her again, and she twisted free again. He scrambled around, got a better grip, and lifted her. She squirmed, nearly toppling them before he could dump her on the bed. He fell on top of her, half on and half off the bed. Both of them were panting from the exertion.

"The floor was perfectly fine," she gasped, struggling to get out from under him.

"No it wasn't." His muffled voice came from somewhere around her stomach. "How many potatoes did you eat at dinner? A hundred?"

She smacked him on the head. "I am not fat!"

"It's all in the jeans, right?"

She began to giggle, helpless to stop herself. His head bobbed up and down with her amusement. She laughed even more at the way they had acted like children.

"Look who's talking." She heaved upward. "I give up. Now will you get off me? You weigh a ton."

He crawled over her to the other side of the bed.

"Ouch! Ouch!" Emily exclaimed as his knee accidentally jabbed her thigh.

"Sorry." He patted her leg. "Good night, Emily. I'd say good night to the rest of the crew, too, but I was never a fan of the Waltons."

He turned his back to her, clearly intent on going to sleep.

She didn't trust him for a second, though, and lay stiffly, ready to leap off the bed the moment he made a move toward her. She debated whether or not to go back to the floor, but decided another tussle could be even more dangerous to her libido. Thank goodness they were both fully clothed.

But Alex didn't move.

As the minutes passed, Emily felt her body relaxing. She mentally stiffened herself, knowing he was just waiting for her to drop her guard before he kissed her. More minutes passed.

Alex didn't move.

She was aware of his body next to her . . . the scent of soap and male . . . the way he radiated heat across the space separating them . . . the line of his shoulders, outlined in the shadowy room, tapering down to narrow waist and hips . . . the length of his legs . . . the sag of the mattress under his weight, pulling her to him in a subtle downward slope . . .

Alex didn't move.

Emily moaned to herself, realizing she was falling under his spell again. She also realized that his deep, regular breathing indicated he was actually asleep. She was torturing herself and he was asleep. The son of a . . .

She bit off the mental curse and concentrated on diversions. Fluffy little sheep leaping over fences. Herself cutting down a tree. Pastoral countryside . . . a stream . . . brilliant green leaves shading her face as she lay on the bank . . . Alex bending over her . . . his mouth touching hers softly, igniting her passions . . .

Emily woke with a snap.

Alex didn't move. Clearly, he hadn't moved from his side of the bed.

She'd been dozing and dreaming in dangerous territory. She knew she ought to get off the bed for her own sake, but was afraid that it would wake him and they'd have another wrestling match. She couldn't risk that, having a good idea of how she would lose. She would just have to lie there, keeping to her side of the bed.

It would be a long night.

"This is as far as I can take you," Jimmy said, stopping his battered truck just outside a village about ten miles from the Greek border.

"Thanks," Alex said, opening the passenger door.

"At least now you look like some poor Greek sod who's out of work," Jimmy told him, grinning. To Emily he added, "And you look like the poor sod's wife, not the all-American girl in blue jeans and ponytail."

Alex was still wearing Jimmy's jeans, along with a pair of work boots. They were a little big, but he was wearing several pairs of socks to compensate. Emily was in a sweater and skirt, clean but not quite matching.

"At least my feet ought to survive this," Alex said. "Jimmy, we can't thank you enough."

"Glad to have my mare and filly alive." He eyed them for a moment. "And I'm glad to help a prince."

Alex froze, half in, half out of the truck.

"Saw your picture on the telly last night," Jimmy went on, "along with the rest of your family after you two went to bed. It's okay, mate. Just tell 'em the truth about what's going on here when you get out. Your grandfather was crazy as hell, but he was right in giving the throne to your aunt."

"I—I don't know what to say," Alex said, touched by the man's words.

"Thank you," Emily said, kissing Jimmy on the cheek. "For everything."

He actually blushed. "I don't know who you are, but you're a helluva woman."

She smiled. "I'm just a tourist. Really."

"And a helluva woman," Alex said, setting his feet on the ground. Emily scooted out behind him. "It's hardly adequate, but thanks, Jimmy."

"Take care. And be careful, you two."

Alex shut the door and Jimmy drove off, kicking up a cloud of dust on the dirt country road.

When they could see the truck no more, Alex and Emily turned in the opposite direction, toward the border.

Eight

Emily felt as if they'd emerged from a warm, safe cocoon and into the cold, cruel world. Jimmy's place had been a haven, and she and Alex had been able to forget their troubles for a little while and laugh together. Somehow that day of camaraderie was more threatening than this.

"Got your flight bag?" he asked.

"Don't leave home without it," she quipped, holding it up for his inspection. He had taken the jewels out the day before and they were back under his shirt. "How long do you think it'll take to get to the border now?"

"About a day."

It was hard to believe that by this time tomorrow it would all be over and she'd be on her way home to Pennsylvania. The question of Alex instantly came to mind, and she just as instantly pushed it out. She didn't want to think that she wouldn't see him again. Instead she thought of the long walk ahead of them. "I don't suppose we could have emerged nice and fresh from Jimmy's truck and still pulled off the poor-souls-without-a-dime-fleeing-back-home routine."

"We won't be able to pull it off if you keep babbling in English."

"Right." She clammed up and walked dutifully one pace behind him in deference to Mediterranean machismo. The thought of machismo reminded her of sex and men, and that reminded her of their playfulness the day before, and that reminded her of the night before that in the hayloft. The images were so vivid, she could actually feel his mouth on her again, sucking . . . nipping . . . driving her into a sensual whirlwind. Desperate to obliterate the memory, she muttered under her breath, "Lions and tigers and bears . . . oh my. Lions and tigers—"

"And knock it off," Alex said, glaring at her.

"Right."

They were nearing the village. Picturesque, Emily thought, eyeing the gray slate roofs, whitewashed walls, and profusion of climbing roses. She could have gone to nice safe Switzerland and seen the same thing. With her luck, though, the Swiss would have rioted over a change in their cheese recipe or something.

As they trudged along, Emily noticed that few people were out, and those who were glanced at them once, then went back inside their homes, closing their doors. By the time they reached the town square, with its three-tiered fountain, the place was absolutely deserted.

She moved closer to Alex and whispered, "Last time I saw something like this, Bela Lugosi was playing the lead."

"They're scared," he said. "A lot of the people in the mountains are superstitious. It's a simple life up here, like night and day compared to the sophisticated jet-setting style along the coast."

"I'll say." She glanced around at the closed doors of the shops. "You'll tell me if my hair crinkles up and the sides go pure white, won't you? If I've turned into the bride of Frankenstein, I want to know it before I look in a mirror."

"And you'll let me know if I grow fangs and start talking with a weird accent."

Somehow their hands met, and Emily wrapped her fingers tightly around his, needing the comfort of flesh to flesh. She shivered in spite of the bright sunlight beating down on her. Even Alex's touch couldn't dispel the eeriness and settle her nerves.

They walked through the village without incident.

"I'm getting paranoid," she finally muttered when they were nearly a half mile up the road.

"I already am," Alex said, sighing in relief. But he pulled her off the road and through the verge until they were safely behind the trees lining the roadway. "I don't like this, people so scared they hide at the sight of strangers. What the hell is Florian doing to create this atmosphere?"

She shook her head. "Fear feeds on itself. It doesn't take much. And to be honest, your aunt and family leaving the country has left them nothing to focus on, to rally behind. What's happening in the city will spread up here soon, though, I'm sure."

"It's always easier to be afraid than to have courage," he said thoughtfully.

"I tell myself that every day before I face twenty five-year-olds."

He chuckled and squeezed her hand. That's when she realized they were still holding hands.

She knew she ought to pull away, but she couldn't. She needed to touch his reassuring presence, to know he was there. She gained strength from it, from the feel of her hand in his. Being dependent on him wasn't as disturbing as she would have thought. In fact, it felt right, very right. She felt . . . whole. Her heart swelled with emotion. Then it sagged with despair at the reminder that once they were across the border, he'd be gone. Then it sagged even further with another thought.

She had fallen in love with him.

The tension in her stomach escalated a thousandfold at the notion. It couldn't be true, she thought desperately, searching her heart and her logic. She couldn't have been that dumb. But she was. Her heart told her so.

"Have you been engaged recently and had it broken off?" she asked, hoping there was some other reason for her reaction.

"No. Why?"

"How about a great love affair gone kaput?"

"Nope."

"A semi-love affair dissolved against your will?"

"Not even close."

"Coveted your neighbor's wife?"

"'Fraid not. Why?"

"Just checking." He didn't seem to be suffering from a broken heart. She had hoped she'd been picking up invisible signals of a love tragedy, and could therefore dismiss her reaction as only sensing the need in him for "tea and sympathy."

She closed her eyes, denying what she was feeling, then opened them in resignation. She wondered how she could have fallen in love with him. When she had fallen.

Probably the moment she found out he was a prince, she thought in disgust. She'd always been a sucker for the Cinderella story. And for someone in trouble. Lord knew Alex qualified on the second score. The eternal maternal had risen again. Combine that with his bravery for taking out the crown jewels, and she was goner.

And she liked him, just plain liked him and enjoyed his company.

That was the worst of all.

"You look funny," he said. "Is anything wrong?"

"Nothing a good dose of stress and burnout wouldn't cure," she replied, positive that would have been better than any vacation. Look at all the trouble she'd gotten herself into on this one.

"That really bothers me," he said pensively. "The village back there, I mean."

"Well, I'm grateful they didn't jump us and drag us away to the police station." She sighed. "And I hope no one is following." She hadn't thought about that until the words popped out of her mouth. "Do you think they are?"

"I doubt it." He turned around, scrutinizing the area behind them. "I don't see anything, and we got off the road as soon as we turned the first bend. If they're hiding because they're scared, why would they follow us?"

Good point, Emily thought. She relaxed a little, but strained her ears for any unusual noises behind them. It seemed to be a habit in Peraco. But she felt sorry for Alex as he walked along, silent and frowning. The villagers' attitude clearly bothered him, and just as clearly had him torn about his old home. He wasn't quite as American as he liked to think he was.

As they put more distance between them and

the village, Emily found her nerves tuning in and tightening up as she considered crossing the border. They had made several horrible mistakes with Jimmy that gave them away. Would they make them again at the border? She and Alex were in no physical harm if they were discovered. But she could be detained, and Alex would be used to give Florian validity. And the coronation would take place.

She wondered if anyone had discovered the jewels missing yet. What would Florian do to the thieves? Maybe they weren't quite as physically safe as she was thinking.

"We're not going to make it past the border," she whispered.

He put his arm around her and hugged her reassuringly. His body's warmth penetrated the sudden chill in hers.

"Yes we will. All we have to do is walk through the woods, past the markers, and we're in Greece."

"Walk through . . . You mean we're not crossing at the checkpoint?"

"Are you crazy?" He raised his eyebrows. "They'd nail us in two seconds. I always planned for us to walk across. We just have to be careful there are no patrols in the area, and we'll have to cope with a fence, I think. But the border's over one hundred miles long, and the patrols can't be everywhere. Under the circumstances, I'm sure the Greeks will forgive us if we don't have an entry stamp."

She nodded, relief washing through her. "Thank goodness nobody's going to ask me anything. I've been worrying about that, knowing my 'bones in the basket' speech is rusty."

"You'd probably get hauled away as a mass murderer if you tried it."

"Macabre humor does not become you," she said. "Well, what's a little fence between friends. Lead on, Macduff!"

"I'm leading, I'm leading."

Even though he let her go after her anxiety attack was over, the atmosphere between them was free and easy. The walking wasn't as onerous as the last time, partly from the full night's rest they'd had and partly because they were out of the steep mountains, where every step was either up or down, straining unused muscles. Maybe tonight they wouldn't have any muscle cramps.

Fear of something else entirely ran down Emily's spine at the thought of no major pain to keep her safe from this emotionally dangerous situation. She shivered and stepped away from the source of her new panic.

"Something wrong?" Alex asked, noticing.

"No." She shook her head and forced herself to smile. "Just . . . thinking."

"Well, we ought to take a break soon. I don't want us to get overtired and have problems when we need them the least."

She nodded again, knowing he made complete sense. Yet a strange and unnerving anticipation crawled through her.

They veered farther away from the road, allowing the woods to swallow them up. Alex finally stopped in the middle of a little glade of pine trees and bracken. Ferns were thick along the ground, and sunlight filtered down in earth-green rays. It seemed a place out of time, offering the peace and isolation that only Mother Nature could provide.

"This place makes you stop and smell the roses

whether you want to or not," Alex said. "It's beautiful."

"No stream at least," Emily muttered. The place reminded her too strongly of last night's sensual dream.

"We don't need a stream," Alex said, patting the bag containing the bottled water. "I've been playing Gunga Din, remember?"

"And a great Sam Jaffe you are." She dropped her flight bag onto the ground and sank down beside it. Eyeing her sneakers, she wondered what her feet looked like. They felt sore, but not overly so. "Do you think it's kinky to be obsessed with one's feet?"

"It'd probably be better to be obsessed with mine rather than your own." He sat down next to her. "Menu's same as the other day. Hope it's all right. Not that we have a choice."

She nodded. "Let's hope I'm not out of breath mints. That salami was stronger than I thought."

They ate leisurely, neither of them in a hurry to continue their journey. Emily found herself wanting to extend this time with him, knowing that once they crossed the border, he would go his way and she hers, back to her sterile nurturing. Much as she loved working with children, she found the idea of returning to her job almost repugnant, simply because she didn't want this to end.

Alex apparently had the same idea, because after lunch he didn't immediately get up. Instead, he stretched out on the ferns, leaning on one elbow. He didn't say anything, just lay next to her. The silence was comfortable, yet held an underlying charge of excitement. Emily found her gaze straying toward his lean legs. The jeans had been slightly baggy, but now were pulled against his flesh, outlining his hard muscles.

Trying to distract herself, she raised her gaze to his chest, knowing that *not* to look at him was even more revealing. His hunched shoulders looked even broader, deepening the taper to his flat torso. She could feel the danger meter creeping toward the red, and wondered if she was becoming a voyeur.

"You said before you lived in Princeton," she began tentatively, hoping conversation would be a cold dousing on her libido. "That's not very far from where I am, you know."

"A couple of hours," he said. "But I'm over here on a year-long project to update the government's computer systems. Even though the electronics are different than the States', the software is alike enough. The biggest problem is converting to the language and personalizing the system for the government's use. I'm overseeing that for them, and my partner's handling the business back home. Computer techs who speak Peracan aren't exactly falling out of trees here."

Her heart fell, however. A whole year. And he hadn't said a word about looking her up when he got back. Instead, he had launched into a lecture.

"Do you have a house or an apartment in Princeton?" she asked, trying to steer things back to home.

"A town house. That made more sense to me than some huge place for just one person." He stared at her. "But it's only been a place to hang a hat. I hadn't realized that before."

"At least there aren't eighty thousand hat racks, like there must be at a palace."

He grinned. "It does have the advantage of

intimacy. You would probably redecorate it in a minute."

"I would?" Her voice squeaked, and she swallowed to wet her throat.

"Sure. You'd load it with cuddlies, maybe a cat motif—"

"I'm not that sappy." She made a face. "I bet it's all antiques and cherrywood."

He raised his eyebrows. "It is. How did you know?"

"Because that's very yuppie. You strike me as very yuppie. Or at least wanting to be."

"And what's in your house?"

"French country," she admitted. "Okay, so you were close."

"I would have been disappointed if I walked in and it was anything else."

His voice was soft, tugging at her senses. She gazed at him. "And will you be walking in?"

He gazed back at her, his eyes becoming intense. "Oh, yes. Will I be invited?"

"Oh, yes."

His mouth sought hers in a soft kiss.

"Have I told you how wonderful you've been?" he asked, his lips against hers.

She dipped her head, almost shyly. "You said I was a helluva woman."

"Unique." He pressed a kiss on the corner of her mouth. "You taste unique too."

"It's the salami," she said, breathless. Her heart was pounding, her blood was singing, and her common sense had already taken a long hike.

"Don't forget the cheese," he murmured.

His mouth claimed hers and every thought fled. She kissed him fervently. Denying him or herself wasn't even an option now. Their tongues twined together, daring and challenging each other in a sensual dance. The scent of him branded her senses, patterning them to remember forever the feel and the shape of him in her mind and heart.

He rolled her onto her back. His chest pressed against her breasts, creating an ache that demanded more than mere satisfaction. Her fingers plunged through his thick hair, the strands gently scoring her palms with more memories. His skin was hot against her cheek, burning with a warmth she'd never forget. The light stubble on his chin grazed her as their lips moved together. When he finally lifted his head, she was gasping with need.

"We shouldn't be doing this," he whispered.

She kissed the side of his mouth. "I know."

Green firs and blue sky buttressed with white clouds soared above his head as his gaze searched hers. "If we don't stop, we won't stop."

She touched her lips to the other corner of his mouth. "I know."

She couldn't stop. She didn't want to. This was her only opportunity to take a memory home, no matter what the pain in the aftermath. Stockholm Syndrome and eternal maternal be damned. His mouth came down on hers like a fire, drawing her up inside the flames. The wanting flared, pushing her against him, every inch of her body melding to his. The thin cotton of her skirt was no barrier, and the lower half of his body pressed heavily on hers. Her hands gripped and tugged as she pulled him as close as possible, trying to absorb him into her skin.

She was vaguely aware of him stripping her sweater and bra from her. He laid her back down, the ferns making a soft bed for her bared flesh. Capturing a nipple in his mouth, he swirled his tongue around the swollen point. She arched into him as his lips roved her flesh, his tongue laving her until she was nearly frantic with the tiny explosions his touch created on her skin. She raised herself up on one elbow, pressing her naked breasts against his face. His eyes were closed, color highlighted his cheekbones, and his expression radiated complete desire. He wanted her.

He reached up and pulled her head down to his. His kiss was devastating, hot and demanding all that she could give. She surrendered herself to it gladly. Her hands desperately tried to get his shirt off, but she couldn't make them work right. He helped her, their mouths never breaking the seal between them. When his bared chest came down on hers, she groaned, the pleasure so intense she thought she would burst from it. She wouldn't survive this, she thought dimly, running her fingers slowly up and down his spine. As she reveled in the feel of smooth flesh and hardened muscles, she didn't want to.

His hand slid up under her skirt, pushing the material away from her legs. It trailed across her thigh, caressing the sensitive inner flesh while his fingers brushed along even softer flesh.

He raised his head. "I want you. Now."

She pulled him back into the kiss, not needing the words, only needing him.

His hands seemed to touch her everywhere, followed by exquisite kisses designed to bring her to the brink of insanity. He pulled the skirt down her legs, and she pushed her sneakers off. His hand skimmed back up, creating a powerful heat. He lifted himself from her only to remove his jeans, her hands helping with the task. She raked her fingers lightly on his buttocks. He moaned and nearly tripped in his haste to get the jeans down the last few inches. She laughed, giving herself over to the feminine power inside her.

He grinned. "You'll pay for that."

"Oh, I hope so," she murmured. She raked her fingers along his body again and watched him suck in his breath at the arousal she evoked. "I truly hope so."

And then all the physical delight of before paled at the incredible sensation of every inch of their skin melting against each other. Alex thought he would go crazy from it, from the feeling of her body under his, in the way he'd dreamed. The way his fantasies had tortured him. He had only wanted to prolong their lunch break, but he had taken one look at her, framed among the green ferns, looking like an earthly dryad tempting him away from his task, and he had been lost.

His fantasies had left out a few details that reality provided, like the incredible silkiness and sweet, sweet scent of her skin. The way she met his kiss and matched it in intensity. The way she arched into him and made funny little noises in the back of her throat when he took her nipple into his mouth. Or the way her leg flexed and her thigh tightened when he ran his hand along them.

She surrendered herself to him without reservation. No woman gave everything, exposed her vulnerability, and exposed it so joyfully, as Emily Cooper did.

He would treasure her and protect her, he vowed as he pressed his hand against the innermost flesh between her thighs. She writhed at his touch, and he drew in a deep breath to control himself . . . and then lost that control when she touched him in kind, exploring the flesh she'd made so hard simply by being. He couldn't wait, he couldn't stop himself from forcing himself into the cradle of her thighs. Her satisfied sigh reached his ears amid the roaring of his blood. Then he plunged himself inside, her satiny folds absorbing him. Both of them gasped at the shock of it, the rightness that could never be denied.

They moved together, giving and receiving. Emily's fingers dug into his back and her legs wrapped around his hips, clinging to him and anchoring him at the same time. He buried his face in her hair, murmuring words that said nothing and everything, as they soared higher and higher toward an abyss of pleasure.

Emily cried out and lifted herself against him, her legs tightening, holding him deep within her even as he joined her in the explosion of burning light and color. It rocked through them, washed over them, and carried them into a sensation-rich darkness.

Slowly, Alex resurfaced, his awareness hampered by a tremendous lethargy. Emily was under him, naked and sheltered. He knew he must be heavy on her, but he couldn't move. He pressed his lips against her throat in apology and decided she tasted more than unique. He didn't know the word for it, and in its current state his brain wouldn't be able to find it even if he did. But she was . . . there was no one like her. No one came close.

He kissed her shoulder in further appreciation, the only action he was capable of at the moment, and she rubbed her foot against his calf. At least he thought it was her foot. It felt . . . scratchy.

"Are you wearing your socks?" he asked.

"Mmm."

He lifted his head and looked back down the length of their bodies. He could see every inch of her flesh seamed to his, not a break in the beautiful creamy-colored skin . . . until his gaze reached the thick white bobby socks slouched around her ankles.

He snorted in amusement, then went back to the pleasurable task of kissing her neck. "You're something, you know that."

"Mmm."

"Can you say anything else?"

She rubbed his back. "Don't want to."

He sighed happily. She didn't regret their lovemaking. He realized he'd been afraid she would. That would have hurt more than he cared to admit. He didn't regret a thing, either, despite having shred his personal oath to be a prince of a gentleman in a battle of need. This was just the beginning . . . once they got out of the predicament they were in.

Reality was beginning to exert itself again, unfortunately. Her leg rubbing was also igniting a spark of magic. Alex told himself to get up and get moving. The sooner they were out of this and the jewels were with his aunt, the sooner he and Emily could get down to the really important things in life. Like having her in his arms on a regular basis.

And not in the woods like two teenagers with nowhere else to go. The ferns couldn't be that soft. Although he would never forget this first time, he vowed that the next time would be in a large bed in the best suite the nearest Hilton had to offer. Emily deserved better than this . . .

She snuggled distractingly against him. "Move your elbow, you're jabbing me in the ribs."

Her words only confirmed his thoughts. He was too heavy. He shifted slightly. "Ah, she speaks."

Her hands fluttered along his shoulders, sending little sensual pulses to his nerve endings. "Do you suppose they made this glade for people like us? It's so beautiful, and there don't even seem to be any bugs. I don't feel any. Do you?"

He smiled, relieved their trysting spot didn't seem to bother her. He tried to concentrate on suggesting they get up, but he didn't want to break their intimacy. "The gods wouldn't allow bugs."

"Maybe Zeus met his Leda here," she said, nuzzling his neck. She kissed his collarbone. "It's very possible, as I'm sure the gods paid no attention to things like borders. Or maybe Apollo met his Artemis here."

"Artemis was a virgin," he said, ready to add that this had all been wonderful, but they needed to move on. Once they were over the border, they could spend all their time in a nice comfortable bed discussing the mating habits of Greek gods.

She sighed and pushed him over onto his back. "Poor Artie. She missed out on a lot."

She was grinning down at him, sly and sexy. Her breasts rubbed against his chest. Alex gave up. This was much more important than saving a country.

He brought her mouth down to his.

Nine

"This can't be it."

Conscious of the fear in Emily's whisper, Alex peered farther into the woods. The twilight shadows created dim illusions amid the trees. "I think so. It's definitely a marker of some kind."

The stick with the sign on it, unreadable from the distance they were at, certainly wasn't a natural part of the forest. They had stumbled upon it unexpectedly, and had immediately leaped behind a big conifer whose branches opened above them like an umbrella.

She pulled a leaf out of her hair. "How many of these are there?"

"Who knows?" He pulled a piece of another one out, grinning at the memory of how it got there.

"You said there was a fence," she reminded him.

"I said I thought there was a fence. There's always one in the movies." He pondered it for a moment. "Fencing is expensive, and these are two friendly countries. People can come and go as they please over the checkpoints. Why would they waste money for a fence? Have the U.S. and Canada fenced every inch of border between them?"

"Actually, I think they have."

He waved a hand in dismissal. "Well, this is Greece and Peraco. We do things differently here. I just wish I could see the sign better, but the light's coming from behind it."

"We should have gotten here earlier, when it was still daylight."

He grinned at her. "We were delayed."

She didn't smile back. "That wasn't my fault."

Uneasiness shot through him that had nothing to do with the border. He searched her face in the dwindling light, then touched her cheek, loving the softness he knew so well now. "I won't excuse our lovemaking, Emily. I wanted you then and I want you now. I won't hurt you. I never would. Are you . . . are you regretting what happened?"

He waited impatiently for her answer, knowing it would either make him ecstatic or hurt him to the bone.

"No," she replied finally. "I will never regret it. But this is no place to talk."

It was the answer he wanted and yet it still hurt somehow. "Emily—"

"Are we going to continue border discussions or are we going to cross the damn thing before someone hears us?"

"We're going, we're going." Much as he wanted to probe further, he knew she was right.

He peered around the area, listening for any unnatural noises. Birds sang and scolded. A breeze ruffled the leaves. Insects chirped. Nothing broke the serenity of the scene.

If they were going, it had to be now. He patted

his shirt to reassure himself the jewels were in place, then took Emily's hand and held it tightly. "We're going to walk like we're out for a Sunday stroll with absolutely nothing to hide."

"I know," she whispered. "It's 'Oh, dear, we're closer to the border than we thought. Silly us.'"

"Right."

Whistling under his breath, Alex stepped out from behind the tree, heading for the barely visible path. His arm stretched out from Emily's . . . and stopped. He tugged. She didn't move.

He whipped around. "Emily!"

"I'm coming," she muttered. She stepped out from behind the tree. Her eyes were wide with anxiety and her gaze darted everywhere.

With a sigh, he started them walking again.

"If anything happens," she said, "I swear I will haunt you for the rest of our unnatural lives."

"I wasn't the one playing, 'Mother, May I?'" he said, walking faster. He realized they were half running and instantly slowed them down. "Walk nonchalant."

"Easy for you to say." But she did walk slower. "See anything?"

"No." They neared the marker. He deliberately veered away from it, walking through the bracken. It snapped under their feet.

"Alex!"

"It's okay. We'll seem even more innocent if we're noisy. Act like we're looking for a spot to make love."

"We found one about five miles back."

He chuckled and put his arm around her waist. Her own arm went around him like a band of steel. "Loosen up. I can't breathe."

"I just want to look like the adoring little woman."

"I should be so lucky." But she did relax the tension in her arm.

They strolled closer to the marker . . . then parallel to it . . . then past it.

"Nobody's leaping out of the bushes and yelling 'Ah-ha!'" Emily whispered hopefully, when the marker was out of sight behind them.

"They don't have to." Alex pointed ahead of them.

The forest was parted violently by a wide strip of denuded land. A road ran down the center of it. Alex stared at it, astonished.

Emily sagged against him. "I think the fat lady just sang."

He took a deep breath. "The hell she did!"

He marched right out into the open, dragging Emily along with him.

"Alex!" she hissed, stumbling over the uneven ground.

"It's just a road," he told her. "All we have to do is walk across it."

And they did. Right straight across without a pause. No one stopped them. No one shouted. No one even appeared. Alex and Emily walked into the woods on the other side of the road and past the marker with the bright blue and white Greek flag insignia.

They had crossed the border without a hitch.

Alex kept them going. They were about a hundred yards onto Greek soil when Emily turned to him.

She whacked him on the shoulder. "Don't ever do that again!"

"Lord, I hope not." He rubbed his shoulder, then

grinned broadly. Suddenly he scooped her up in his arms, spun her around, and kissed her soundly. "We did it! Emily, we did it!"

She laughed. "No thanks to you scaring me nearly to death."

"It's good for your heart," he said, then set her on her feet. "You're squishing the you-know-what."

Her cheeks flushed bright red.

He roared with laughter. "Not that! The other family jewels. I better get you to the nearest Hilton. Who knows what you'll do with your dirty mind."

"Very funny," she said. "I promise not to jump your bones. Happy now?"

"No."

She smiled sweetly. "Can we go before a Greek patrol decides to throw us back?"

"Chicken." But he took her hand and led them on.

He wondered how deep the woods were on this side of the border. There weren't open meadows right at the border, and that wasn't promising as far as nearby civilization was concerned. He calculated they had walked nearly an hour when they finally emerged from the woods. A road of fresh tarmac wound its way in front of them.

He glanced at her and held out his arm. "Shall we walk?"

"Absolutely."

She linked her arm in his and they strolled off down the road . . . and strolled and strolled.

"My feet hurt," Emily complained about an hour later.

Alex peered ahead, trying to see even a farm-house. He didn't hope for a village.

When another mile brought nothing, he began to give up all hope, deciding they'd have to walk all the way to Athens. But they rounded a bend and came upon open fields as far as they could see. The change was abrupt in the way only man could make. A lonely farmhouse sat off the road.

"Civilization!" he exclaimed.

They walked up to the old, scarred wooden door and Alex knocked. It opened slightly to allow a man to peer out.

"*Yassas, Kyriós,*" Alex began in Greek. "Please, can you tell us where is the nearest inn?"

The door opened wider and a youngish man stood framed in the threshold. A gaggle of children burst out of the house and crowded around them, giggling and chattering in excitement. Clearly, visitors were a treat.

"What are they saying?" Emily whispered to Alex.

His heart stopped at her words. Then he sighed in relief as he remembered they were in Peraco no longer, so it didn't matter if Emily spoke English.

"Are you English?" the man asked. "I heard your wife. I speak a little."

Alex hesitated, then nodded. "We're lost and looking for the nearest inn or hotel."

"I will . . . speed you in my . . . how you say . . . truck," the farmer said in English, beaming proudly. The truck seemed a prized possession. So was his English.

"*Efharisto,*" Alex said, thanking him. He turned to Emily. "He'll take us to an inn."

"Faster than a speeding bullet too," she quipped.

"Come in, come in," the farmer said. "Have something to drink and eat before I take you."

"Thank you," Alex said again, and ushered Emily into the inviting warmth inside.

"Stay on the roadways around here," the farmer went on in Greek as he shut the door. Clearly, he had exhausted his little bit of English. "We're close to the border here and those crazy Peracans are patrolling everywhere. They've also begun putting in mines. It's terrible! Our sheep had grazed across here for centuries, with only a little fence between. But now try and send your flock to the lower meadows and it's 'Ba-boom!'" The farmer flung up his hands in a vivid demonstration.

Alex stared at the man. The room dimmed to near black and a cold sweat broke out on his forehead. He and Emily had walked across the border, wandered around it, and could have been . . .

The scarred road hadn't been a road, but the preparations for mining the area. By sheer luck, they'd missed the patrols. And if they had crossed a few days later or farther south . . . He didn't even want to think of it.

"What's he saying?" Emily asked.

Alex pulled himself together. "That the dog likes digging holes."

"Oh."

If only she knew, he thought, and he vowed never to tell her. He could just imagine what her "ba-boom" would be.

Emily halted just inside the bedroom the small tavern in Loutros provided. The stuccoed walls were painted a gleaming white. Ragged thin black curtains, reminiscent of World War Two black-out drapes, hung from the tiny window high above a warped sea chest. The only wall adornment was a crucifix above the lumpy-looking bed. A rag rug the size of a bar of soap lay on the near side, waiting for a misplaced foot to begin the wild ride across the polished wood floor.

Emily focused on the other person in the room. She knew she ought to say something, protest their continuing the husband-and-wife disguise, tell Alex that what had happened in the woods was a once-in-a-lifetime event, that she didn't expect anything more, emphasize again that she didn't *want* or expect anything from him. But her tongue was frozen to the roof of her mouth.

"The bed's small," he said, stripping off his jacket. "And it's not the Hilton, but it's clean. We'll manage."

"Actually . . ." Her voice cracked. She cleared her throat. "I think it would be better if we had separate rooms."

He sat down on the bed and eyed her sourly. "I knew it. From the moment we left that glade, you've been cold and distant. If you worried that we were unprotected—"

"I'm not," she said. "Well, I am, and it's another reason why we shouldn't be sharing a room together, but that isn't my main concern right now. It's the fact that it *did* happen at all."

"I thought you said you didn't regret it."

"I don't."

"You don't act it. In fact, I've never seen anyone act *more* regretful than you." His gaze narrowed. "We made love. We were as intimate as a man and woman can ever be, and afterwards you treat me like I'm an ogre."

"I don't mean to." She steeled herself against his hurt. "Alex, I told you I didn't want a vacation fling, and I still don't. What happened happened, but there can never be anything between us. You know it as well as I do. We aren't even close on things in common. I'm just trying to act like a grown-up about this and acknowledge the inevitable."

There, she thought. She'd said it, done the right thing, recognized reality with a mature decision. She believed him when he said he wouldn't hurt her, and he wouldn't set out to. But his honor code would demand that he continue a relationship with her for her sake. Her honor code demanded she forbid it for his.

He got up and walked across to her. He loomed over her, not touching her, yet effectively trapping her all the same. She flattened her back against the door to give herself breathing space. Literally. He was having his usual effect of taking all the air out of the room. A vise squeezed her lungs and she gasped for air.

"Emily, what's really wrong?" he asked softly.

"I told you," she squeaked.

"I don't believe it." He reached out and traced her cheek with his forefinger. "How can you deny this?"

"It isn't enough," she whispered. "It never will be."

His hand dropped away. She could still feel the trail of sensuality he'd left on her skin.

"I know we were thrown together," he said, "that everything is a mess right now." He paused. "I feel like all I have is you."

"But how long will it last?" she forced herself to ask. She refused to say what she was really feeling for him. She couldn't afford to expose her emotions that way. And he would really feel honor-bound to make a relationship then.

He smiled slightly. "Why can't you let it grow and see where it will go?"

"I'm being sensible, Alex." For once in her life, she added silently. "Why can't you accept that?"

"Oh, hell!" He spun away angrily and grabbed his jacket. "I'll go find another room."

She stepped aside from the door. He whipped it open, stepped out, and slammed it shut behind him. The crucifix tilted precariously. Dust shifted down from the rafters above.

Okay, so he wasn't a happy camper, she thought. Neither was she.

Several hours later, she lay in the small, hard, lumpy bed, still feeling depressed. Even her phone call home hadn't buoyed her up for long. She'd smiled as her mother cried, "What took you so long? You used to sneak in and out after your curfew all the time, so why couldn't you sneak out of a country faster than this? Don't think your father and I didn't know. Omigod, Emmy, I was so scared." It had been good to hear their voices, good to know she was out of an unpleasant situation and almost on her way back to Pennsylvania. So why did her brain keep turning back to the last few days of desperation? Why did that seem to be the best time of her life? It shouldn't. It shouldn't. But it did.

Noises from the tavern downstairs filtered up through the floorboards as the occupants celebrated life in true Greek tradition. The Greeks also thought it quite sensible to celebrate until the wee hours all night every night. It wasn't the laughter, Emily thought, flipping over to avoid yet another lump. It was the wailing music with its distinct

Arabic flavor. The Asia Minor influence that had missed Peraco was more prevalent here. And at one in the morning, it had the effect of fingernails across a blackboard. Worse, the curtains were strictly for decoration and wouldn't close over the window. Bright lights streamed into the room.

If only she could sleep, Emily thought, closing her eyes tightly against the lights. Insomnia was getting to be her middle name. And one man seemed to have caused that condition. If only she could forget . . .

Someone pounded on her door, and she jumped, her heart thumping painfully.

"Emily!"

Panic shot through her at the urgent tone of Alex's voice.

"What? What?" She threw on a shirt to cover the underwear she was wearing, then scurried over to the door and flung it open. "What?"

Alex slipped inside. "How did your phone call go earlier? Is everyone at home all right?"

She stared at him. "You nearly broke down the door and scared me for that?"

"Oh." He shrugged. "I didn't think you would hear me over the noise downstairs."

"Well, I wasn't asleep," she said, also shrugging.

"Everyone at home all right?" he asked again.

"Yes."

"I guess they were glad to hear from you."

She nodded. "My dad said my class made a big picture of me and signed it, then sent it to the President to ask him to get me back. Gregory Morris suggested they trade Michael Jordan for me."

Alex laughed. "I wonder what Michael Jordan would say."

"No deal, I'm sure." She smiled. "But I'm proud of Gregory. He's a big Jordan fan. I'm proud of all of them. Did you get in touch with your aunt?"

"No. Not yet. I thought it would be better to wait until we get to Athens. I asked around casually downstairs if they knew exactly where she might be in exile here. One man heard she's staying on Oinousai, with one of her Greek shipping magnate friends. That figures. Oinousai is a Greek island just off the coast of Turkey." He grinned. "We should have gone out the other side."

"Great," Emily muttered, recognizing another out-of-her-world difference between them. When her aunt traveled, she stayed at the Holiday Inn. His stayed with billionaires. "I suppose you'll be going there right away."

"As soon as we get to Athens."

"Oh."

He took a step toward her and touched her cheek. She desperately wanted to lean into his caressing fingers. Instead, with considerable effort, she tilted her face away.

"Why can't you give us a chance?" he asked.

"I told you."

"That's not enough." He pulled her to him. "Emily, what are you afraid of? What have I done to push you away?"

"Nothing. Don't ever think that," she whispered, pressing her face against his shirt. "But Alex, after we get to Athens, you'll be going your way and I'll be going mine. I can't see causing myself more pain."

He lifted her chin and gazed down at her. "Emily, I'm not going my way. I'm going wherever you go for as long as you'll let me."

His mouth came down on hers. She'd wanted his kiss so badly, she couldn't resist it. The moment she'd let him in the room, she'd known this would happen. His lips held pleasure and promise, and all the emotionally correct words fell away as her starved senses took over. She knew that no matter what her good intentions, this was what she craved. If only he meant what he said, she thought.

A little voice inside her asked, *What if he did?* The temptation was tremendous. Stronger women than she had fallen to the thought.

He lifted his head. "Emily, I can't be without you."

His second kiss, combined with those words, was more than her crumbling resolve could control. She gave herself up to the silken bonds already between them.

The lumpy bed miraculously smoothed itself out as they made love. Emily straddled him, sheathing him in her flesh, surrendering herself gladly. No regrets, her mind chanted softly in time to the ancient rhythms they created.

There were none to be had.

The bus to the coast city of Alexandropoúpolis was crowded and hot, and the engine belched black smoke and raw diesel every time the driver fed it gas. The old twin-engine ferry plane to Athens wasn't much better, the updrafts over the blue Aegean Sea bouncing the craft like a yo-yo.

Alex sighed when they finally landed in Athens's thoroughly modern, very international airport. At least he and Emily weren't out there on their own any longer. Now that the fear of being caught with the jewels was past, he decided they could give a few essentials priority.

"First," he said, "a hotel and some sleep—"

"And a shower," Emily added.

The picture of the two of them naked in the shower, with water running down their bodies, flashed into his mind. "Right. A *long* shower. And then the embassy." He put his arm around her as they walked across the runway.

"Yours or mine?"

"Ours."

"Sorry, I forgot."

"Well, don't." He squeezed her against his side. "I'm as American as apple pie."

"It's just the tree that's halfway around the world, right?"

He made a face. "Okay, so I've fallen a little farther than the edge of the field."

She poked him in the ribs. "I'm teasing you. If you were any more American, Michael Jackson would be handing over his spangled glove."

The old Emily was back, he thought happily. Teasing and at ease with him. And at ease now with their intimacy. All he had to do was turn over the jewels to his aunt and his obligation to the "tree," as Emily put it, was done.

The moment they were in a taxi, Alex told the driver, "The nearest Hilton." He added to Emily, "I have this dream."

"Naturally."

The dream was nearly undone by the desk clerk asking for their passports. Alex plunked down on the marble countertop the ones Tuno had had made, while silently cursing himself for forgetting most hotels' practice of holding a guest's passport. The clerk didn't even blink, though, and tucked the packets away for safekeeping. Alex decided they were on a definite roll.

Once they were inside the room, Emily spun around and flung herself on the bed. "Made it!"

Alex walked over to the foot of the mattress and wedged his legs between her knees. "The heart of civilization."

She gazed up at him, her expression amused. "You didn't think we would get by with those passports. I saw your face."

"I knew there was no problem," he lied.

"Sure you did." She sat up and began to toy with his shirt buttons. "We're going to sleep now, right?"

"Eventually." He bent her back across the bed, keeping his body hovering just above hers.

"You forgot to say that before," she murmured, batting her eyelashes. "You said food and sleep and a long shower. You didn't say anything about making love. Really, you need to make these things clear, Alex."

"I'll do better."

And he did.

Ten

"You didn't tell him about the jewels," Emily said.

They were standing outside the American Embassy in downtown Athens, and Alex was staring away from her, his jaw set.

In the distance the skyline was dominated by the seat of ancient Western civilization. The Acropolis loomed above the city, the marbled columns of the Parthenon gleaming white in the bright sunlight. The temple crowned the hillside like a jewel in a rough setting. Today, however, it held no allure.

She prompted him further. "They'd be safe in the embassy."

"Would they?" He turned and looked at her. "Or would the government have an obligation to turn them back over to Florian? They are the property of Peraco. It doesn't matter who's in charge."

"I hadn't thought of that."

"The truth is, I don't know who to trust. I think it's just best if I take them directly to my aunt. She's the rightful heir, and she can handle it from there."

"It makes sense to me." And it also kept him with her a little longer, she thought. The end of their quest was rushing up at her like an apocalyptic horseman, and she had no idea how to stop it.

Even as she thought that, guilt washed through her. She had chucked all her good intentions of keeping their relationship platonic out of selfishness, because her need far outran her common sense. But she couldn't help herself, couldn't shut the wanting off like a faucet. She knew the thought of Princess Emily was a ridiculous one. It was right out of "Mr. Rogers' Neighborhood." In real life, it wasn't even a remote possibility.

But she had to be with him for as long as she could. And when it was time for her to go, she would slink off into the sunset without looking back. But she couldn't do the right thing now. She couldn't. Not when she loved the wrong thing so badly.

Alex's sigh brought her attention back to him. "It would be nice to get these things out from under my shirt," he said. "If I ever took my jacket off, I'd look like that guy from the movie *Alien*. Any minute now I expect a crown prince to erupt from my side."

"But we're not telling anybody."

"No. I've got to see it through to the end."

In a way she was glad, but his anger and frustration were growing. And his words had an ominous ring to them, as if he meant more than bringing the jewels to safety.

A bad feeling crept over her, but she dismissed it and leaned against him. "There's only one solution to any problem."

"Sex?"

"No, silly. Shopping. I need some new underwear anyway."

"Can you get the kind that's all lacy?" he asked, perking up.

She grinned. "Is there any other?"

"Well, yes. There's silk . . . and satin . . . and edible . . ."

"It's not me who's getting kinky now," she said, taking the lead and dragging him along. "Let's go before you get worse."

"We've shopped 'till we've dropped," Emily said hours later, plopping into one of the chairs in their room. She peered down at her aching feet. "You'd think these things attached to my legs would be used to walking by now. They've done enough of it lately."

But not much more, she couldn't help thinking. They'd told her at the embassy that morning that her new passport would be issued in a day or two. Then she would return home. Alex would be leaving for Oinousai even sooner than that, although he hadn't said exactly when. She didn't even want to think about it. She had twenty-four hours at least, and she wanted full advantage of them. With no regrets. No Stockholm Syndrome, no worrying about their affair being only that. No nothing. Just him and her.

He set the bags on the bed. "I'm surprised you didn't buy more, Emily. Just a dress and some tops and pants aren't enough."

"Yes, they are. For now. I'll get more if I have to, once I get my replacement credit card from the bank here."

He rounded on her. "Do you mean you didn't get more because *I* was buying?"

She hesitated, then plunged on. "Yes, Alex. You've paid for enough already."

His face flushed a dull red. "Dammit, Emily, do you have to fight me at every single level?"

"Isn't it more exciting?" she asked, smiling at him while hoping to diffuse his wrath.

"Hell, no! I'm really tired of this damned independent attitude American women have."

"Alex, I think you've been in Machismo Land too long. And the hot sun. Your brains are fried."

"No, they're not." He pointed a finger at her. "And I am not being macho about this, either! It's silly to be so stiff-necked about your involvement with me that you won't even buy enough clothes."

"But I have bought enough clothes," she said in a calm voice.

"No you haven't. You just said so."

Emily groaned. He *had* been in Machismo Land too long. She should have recognized his need to provide for her and backed down on her principle for once. Heck, she could have sent him a check afterward, right? Now it was too late.

She wished she were being grilled in some basement of the consulate, rather than fighting with him. Even torture was more appealing than wasting their time together on another shopping trip just to salve his bruised ego.

"Alex, I have enough clothes," she said firmly, knowing she had to diffuse any such thought before it occurred to him. "I'm sorry I offended you. I never meant to. Tomorrow, *when* my feet are better, I will take your card and spend until the account number is worn off the damn thing. Are you happy now?"

He frowned. "Barely."

Alex was being irrational and he knew it. He cursed under his breath. To appease some ego thing, he was wasting precious time with Emily. But a pressure cooker had been heating inside him over the last weeks, and it had erupted today. Stupid, he thought. Next time he had an urge to listen to his caveman half, he'd get a pair of ear plugs. What did it matter whose card she used?

It mattered.

"Please tell me we're not going anywhere else," she said, clearly reading the expression on his face.

"We're here to stay," he promised.

"I'm glad about that. And you don't have to look so unhappy."

"I'm not unhappy." He shrugged. "In fact, I'm about to make a big apology. I was silly."

"Well, you had to yell about something."

"Thanks for being magnanimous. Do you want your feet rubbed?"

She lifted them onto the edge of the mattress. "Be my guest."

He sat down on the bed and picked up her foot, setting it on his lap. He began to rub, feeling the stiffness of her muscles through the stocking. He could also see the long line of leg under her skirt, nearly to the top of her thigh. A little secret voyeurism never hurt anyone, he told himself happily while admiring the view.

"You haven't said when you're leaving to see your aunt," Emily commented, resting her head against the back of the chair. Her eyes were already closed.

"I know. The truth is I ought to go right away,

but I want to see you safely on your plane home first."

She was silent for a moment, a funny look on her face. "You don't have to do that."

He stared at her, drinking in her features. "I want to do that. I need to, Emily."

She opened her eyes and gazed at him for one long moment.

"What you have is more important than me," she whispered.

"No, it isn't."

He leaned over and gently kissed her. Her mouth was like fine wine, a blending of tangibles that created an intangible, addicting taste.

He pulled back finally and concentrated again on making her feet more comfortable.

"What are you going to do after you take the jewels to your aunt?" she asked.

That thought had been niggling at the back of his brain for days now. Just going back to the States didn't seem right anymore. He shrugged. "I don't know. Come home after you."

"Oh."

He realized he'd made it sound as if it were a prison sentence. Grinning, he added, "Of course I would come home after you. I meant, I don't know what will happen with the job over here. It's a wait and see if Julia can regain the country."

"Oh," she said again, but she looked relieved.

Still, he sensed something was bothering her. "What's wrong?" He began to stroke her leg. "I know. I have to convince you of my sincerity."

"No, no. You're sincere."

"It's more fun to convince you." He pulled her up and laid her on the bed, then set the bag of clothes on the floor.

She leaned over the edge of the bed, staring down at the bag. "I wonder how I'm going to wear them all in one day, just to make you happy."

The graceful line of her back and the curve of her derriere caught his eye. It was too much.

He sprawled on top of her and forgot about clothes and crown jewels and airline tickets and leaving unfinished business behind.

This was so much better.

"Well, there it is. One plane ticket home," Emily said, flipping the travel itinerary folder in her hand. "Nice of the government to arrange to get me on one in twenty-four hours. Our tax dollars at work."

Alex glanced at it, then away, preferring to look at anything else in the American Express Travel Office than the thing that would separate them tomorrow night. He desperately wanted to ask her to stay, but knew that would be incredibly selfish on his part. She had a family and a classroom full of children worried about her and waiting for her. He'd catch up in a few days.

The thought of what he would be leaving behind also tore at him. Tuno . . . Stanni . . . Pieter, who risked so much to get the coronation jewels out . . . the transplanted English farmer . . . the men from his office. He felt as if he were turning his back on them somehow, just walking away and not giving a fig about them or anyone else. That little village where Jimmy had dropped them off had been haunting him, too, its contrast so stark to the freewheeling, open lifestyle here in Greece. The only contrast within Peraco should be between its jet-set beaches and quaint, picturesque mountain villages. What caused those villagers' fear had created a deepening anger inside him, a burning fuse dangerously close to a powder keg.

Something else went even deeper, the feeling that no matter where he lived, Peraco was still his home. He had more obligation to join against the coup than most. It was a family affair. And family mattered. He could see that now.

His uncle had to be stopped, and Alex knew he couldn't just walk away from that. He couldn't face Emily, either, if he did nothing.

She slipped the travel folder and ticket in her ever-present flight bag, then tucked her hand in the crook of his elbow and nudged him toward the doors. They walked out into the mild evening air, people bustling around them on their way to the local cafes for Greece's "second day."

"I guess we didn't have to buy you so many clothes," he said glumly.

"Sure we did." Her encouraging smile didn't quite reach her eyes. "You wouldn't want me to go naked, would you?"

"I'll have to think about that." He put his arm around her. She was warm and real against his side, their hips bumping slightly as they walked. "I wish you weren't going."

"You do?"

"Yes, I do." He sighed, then smiled. "But you have to. You have a lot of people back home who've been scared for you. You can't stay just to appease me. I'll take care of this last little piece of business and be along a day or two after you. We can manage that."

He'd said the right thing, and it actually felt good. He would never feel right if he tried to keep her with him. Just as he'd never feel right leaving others behind to fight his uncle.

"I don't want to manage it," she said.

He chuckled. "Is this the same woman who pleaded, wheedled, and actually tried to run away from me back at Tuno's?"

A reluctant giggle escaped her. "The same."

"I can't keep you here," he said, sobering. "Not when there are others so worried about you."

"They're not worried anymore. They know I'm all right."

He couldn't let her go. Never. "Will you . . . will you stay with me and take the jewels to my aunt's?"

She took a deep breath and smiled. "I'd thought you'd never ask. Of course I'll stay. You'd probably be lost without me."

He kissed her soundly. "That's an understatement."

He gazed down at her. He'd never felt so pleased and fulfilled before. It was an odd thought, but he realized that had been an elusive element to his life. He'd never felt fulfilled before.

Except even now, with the woman he loved—and he did love her—beside him, he was aware of an emptiness as he thought of Peraco.

He ignored the sensation. He had Emily and it ought to be enough for now. He was determined it would be. Always.

After a late dinner and a little bit of ouzo, they went back to the hotel. As he swung open the door to their room, Alex decided he would make this a night to remember for both of them.

And they did.

Eleven

"Any bad guys? Emily asked, forcing herself to be cheerful as she leaned over the ferry's railing and looked at the disembarking passengers.

They had arrived on Oinousai, a tiny island off the larger Chios and home to some thirty Greek shipping families. Their palatial homes dotted the seaward cliffs of the island, bleached white from the relentless Mediterranean sun.

"Who the hell can tell?" Alex muttered, staring at the houses and shops along the dock.

She sensed his withdrawal, had been sensing it for a while now. He was unhappy about something, and she had her suspicions about what it was.

"Mrs. Pollifax?" she asked, trying to lighten his mood.

"They all look like Mrs. Pollifax," he grumbled, watching a band of older women fuss their way up the dock.

"No kidding. I never saw so many little old lady tourists in my life."

Alex held them back until they were the last ones off the ferry. They walked down the gangway and into the small port village. Its streets wound back toward the interior of the island, leading upward onto the island plateau.

Emily forced herself to smile and act unconcerned. But it was only an act. Alex had been increasingly quiet since they'd left Athens, and it had taken her most of the ferry trip to finally figure out why.

He was going back to Peraco. She was terrified at the thought. He wouldn't be safe. But how could she persuade him not to do the noble thing? She couldn't even find the words. On a personal level, she recognized another factor. Going back would be his graceful way of breaking with her. She had dared to hope, but she should have known.

She had always been aware that this was just a moment in time for Alex. But she had been so caught up in the eternal maternal and the Stockholm Syndrome, she'd set herself up for this fall. It had waited for her here at Oinousai, right at the end.

She would never survive without him.

"Julia's staying with Constantine Lemos," Alex said, taking her arm.

This would be the last walk with Emily for a while, he thought. Though just a little while. In the meantime he wanted her closeness, the feel of her soft skin, the scent of her filling his nostrils before he told her what he had to do.

"Lemos," she repeated. "Like that island we passed earlier?"

He nodded.

"He's got a whole island named after him and he lives on Oinousai?"

"That's because Oinousai is the 'in' place to live. Lemos isn't named after him. It's his family name."

"Bet they lived there once. So how do we get there?"

He cleared his throat. She would hate the answer.

She groaned. "Walk. I knew it."

"You've rested all day on the boat," he reminded her.

"So quit complaining and let's get moving," she finished, hiking her flight bag up on her shoulder and walking faster along the dock.

Alex caught up with her and put his arm around her waist. They strolled past the cars waiting at the street's edge, drivers lounging on the hoods. A few people, all tourists, were out for the ritual evening stroll along the waterfront before they began a night of partying in the local taverna to celebrate *kefi*, that sense of well-being Greeks so loved.

Alex wished he had a little *kefi* at the moment as he surveyed each person they passed. Instead, he had the other side of the Greek nature: *anisichia*. He just couldn't shake that feeling of worry— disquiet—as they slowly made their way out of town. They were so vulnerable, like being naked. He loved being naked with Emily, but this wasn't what he had in mind.

"Which house is it?" she asked, glancing behind them.

He paused. "The biggest."

She halted, frowning at him. "You don't know, do you?"

"Well . . . no."

"This is wonderful. I thought you knew."

"I've never been here before, actually," he admitted. "I know a bit from family talk, but I don't know exactly which house is his. I meant to ask in town."

She began to turn around, but he pulled her back.

"Forget it. I'm not crazy about going back and asking around. That will attract attention. We'll just knock on some doors."

"If we can get past the Dobermans. Laurel and Hardy could do a better job, Alex."

"I thought we were more like Nick and Nora Charles."

"You're no William Powell."

"Fussy. Come on."

He linked her arm through his and guided her along the side of the roadway. The farther they got from town, the more his *anisichia* receded. They had come so far, through so much, it was impossible they wouldn't finish their task. His anticipation rose with each step.

On the plateau the road still dipped and turned sharply, the land being riddled with the occasional steep slope. The first few homes were on the small side, and two had initials on their gates, neither an *L*. They walked deeper into the island's interior, passing no one on the road.

"I feel like I'm back in that Bela Lugosi movie," Emily said, moving closer to him.

"It's still early for people to be out and about. Besides, this is supposed to be a getaway spot."

She looked around. "Getaway from where?"

"Everywhere else."

They rounded a bend toward the far end of the

island . . . and found themselves facing a man on the deserted road. He held a gun. Alex tensed, cursing himself for being relaxed rather than vigilant. The man hadn't just popped out of nowhere. He must have cut across the headland, rather than up the road.

The man was tall and dark. He inclined his head. "Your Highness. I believe we need to . . . talk."

"I don't think so," Alex said, trying to watch the man's eyes and hands and his own mouth at the same time.

"This tears it!" Emily suddenly exclaimed. "The vacation of a lifetime turns into a coup, then I walk a thousand miles in lousy shoes and deliver a horse. Now I'm going to be shot on a Greek millionaire's playground. Just what the hell is this?"

"It's called irony, my love," Alex said, half amused at the gunman's gaping expression. Emily did have the ability to leave one speechless.

But he knew her blowup had been designed as a distraction.

Out of the corner of his eye he spied a gap that sloped downward and away from the road. If they could reach it, they could get lost in the island's nooks and crannies, or reach the beach near the town. Frantically, he wondered how he could turn the man's surprise to his advantage. Unfortunately, the gun didn't waver in the man's hand. Alex would risk himself, but he'd never risk Emily.

She turned on him. "Irony, my a—"

"Enough!" the gunman snarled. "Your uncle is very disappointed in you. He wishes to have his property returned, and he asked me to assure you that all will be forgiven."

It was a prepared speech. Alex didn't trust it for a minute. The one edge they had was that the man would not hurt them. There would be terrible repercussions if anything happened to him. In fact, it was in the man's best interest to ensure nothing did happen.

The gunman shifted meaningfully. "Your Highness, please. Let's not be foolish. You can be charged with theft of a national treasure . . . and treason. You wouldn't want that for yourself. Or your lovely companion."

So that was how his uncle planned to play it, Alex thought.

"Very suave," Emily said, smiling sweetly. "Don't you get anything but James Bond here?"

"Emily," Alex warned. Facing twenty kindergartners every day had made her too brave. "All right. I can see we have no choice. Give him your flight bag, Emily."

She turned and gaped at him in bewilderment. "My flight bag?"

"Your flight bag," he said between clenched teeth.

"My . . . flight . . . bag," she repeated slowly, as realization dawned.

A low rumble reached their ears from behind the man. A car was coming along the road.

The man snapped his fingers. "Give it here. Now!"

Emily let the strap drop slowly from her shoulder.

"Hurry!" He waved the gun. His eyes betrayed his inner anxiety.

She held out the bag just as the car rounded the bend behind them.

Alex grabbed her arm and pulled her along with

him as he raced for the gap. The man shouted and cursed, and the car's horn blared loudly as brakes screeched.

"Why didn't you give him the damn bag?" Alex asked, veering to the left. The slope dropped sharply toward the sea.

"I was trying to," she panted, as they slid down the rocky earth, kicking up dust and pebbles as they went.

"You were taking your time about it."

"Aren't you glad?"

"Yes. But don't do it again!"

At the bottom of the short cliff, Alex steered her toward town. They got only about a hundred yards when they ran headlong into an abrupt lack of land. They skidded to a halt.

"Now what?" she asked.

He spun around, but to their right was a sheer cliff face and to their left it was straight down to the sea and jagged rocks. Forward was more sea and back . . .

Back, the man was walking steadily toward them.

Emily immediately held out the flight bag. "Here it is."

He snatched it out of her hands and smiled coldly at them. "Thank you, Your Highness. And thank you for our little jog. This is more private for us. First, I'll check for the package . . ."

He knelt and emptied the contents of the bag, his eyes never leaving them. His free hand felt around for a moment, then he glanced down. In a second he saw what wasn't there, and he rose to his feet, his expression colder than ever.

"It's not here!" He kicked at the pile. Cards, books, flashlight, scarf, makeup kit, skin cleanser/flea killer—everything except the crown jewels—flew everywhere.

"That was very foolish," he said. "Now, where are the crown jewels?"

Alex shrugged. Emily squeezed his hand tightly.

The man stepped forward menacingly. Suddenly he was knocked over as a body barreled into him. The gun went flying as their rescuer wrestled with the man and overpowered him.

Alex picked up the gun and trained it on his uncle's henchman. A tousled Stanni knelt on the man's back, grinning triumphantly.

"My leg!" the man howled. "I think you've broken it!"

"Sorry," Stanni said cheerfully.

"Where did you come from?" Alex asked. "Not that I'm ungrateful."

"I've been with your aunt for days, waiting for you and Emily," Stanni said while patting the man down. He yanked the man's jacket down around his arms to immobilize him. His and Alex's belts finished the job at the wrists and ankles.

Emily sank down on a rock. "I think I'm going to be sick."

"Are you okay?" Alex asked, giving the gun to Stanni.

"Yes," she said, nodding. "It's nothing thirty years of staying home won't cure."

"We'll be home for forty years," Alex promised.

"Well, well," Stanni said as he stared down at the man. "I believe he's one of your uncle's personal bodyguards. I've seen him hanging around the island for several days now and presumed he might be waiting for you. No matter. He's not going anywhere for now. Come along. You two have something to finish."

"We're leaving him?" Alex asked.

The man cursed loudly.

Stanni sighed. "For the moment. We'll send back the police. They don't like people assaulting Mr. Lemos's guests."

Alex helped Emily to her feet, then took her in his arms, feeling the chill in her lithe body. He embraced her tightly to chase away the shudder that ran through her and to reassure himself that she was all right. He was never so grateful for the feel of her against him. Her hair smelled of roses and wildflowers, her flesh was like satin, and her body fit perfectly to his. It always would.

Stanni cleared his throat. "If you don't mind . . ."

Alex raised his eyebrows. "I do. But we'll go anyway."

Arm in arm, they walked past the man, giving him a wide berth. Stanni followed behind, saying, "Someone will be back in just a little bit. I suggest you stay put, otherwise you're likely to do more damage to yourself and have a very slow recovery."

The man called Stanni several things that Alex didn't bother to translate for Emily. She didn't ask. She really didn't need to.

Once they were back on the road, Stanni said, "Lemos's estate is about a half mile farther. You two shouldn't have any problem reaching it—"

"Aren't you coming with us?" Emily asked.

Stanni smiled wryly. "Someone has to notify the police about our friend. Then I must leave and go back to Peraco. My job was to keep Alex safe. That's done now."

"Keep me safe?" Alex echoed.

Stanni shrugged, looking oddly vulnerable and boyish. "Your aunt's been worried for some time about Florian's intentions, so I was assigned to watch you. She says you're the only sane one in the family and therefore valuable."

Alex gaped at him. It was hard to believe Stanni, seemingly fresh out of college, was much more than he seemed.

"But you didn't come with us before," Emily said. "You took the car back."

"Because it was easily traced to Tuno and showed which way you went," Stanni explained. "You were safe enough in the mountains, and it was an easy crossover to Greece."

"Want to bet?" Alex muttered, remembering the Greek farmer's warnings.

"I figured I'd wait here for you," Stanni continued. "I knew you'd come eventually. Although I nearly missed that one when he disappeared from his permanent table at the beach taverna. I followed him as he followed you."

"The cat following the mice following the cheese," Emily said.

The ferry whistle sounded its first departing signal.

Stanni listened as the sound faded, then smiled at them. "Tell your aunt I'm going back. If I miss this ferry, it will be three days before the next one comes. They need help on the inside now. It is my home and my princess. I must defend them as my ancestors have for a thousand years." His smile became a grin. "It's a helluva burden."

Emily disengaged herself from Alex and hugged the younger man. "Take care of yourself."

Alex opened his jacket and pulled out the jewels. He shoved the velvet bag into Emily's hands.

"Take them to my aunt," he said, then hauled her back into his embrace and kissed her soundly.

"Alex!" she exclaimed when he released her.

The ferry whistle blew a second warning, its urgency easily recognized.

He kissed her again. "I have to go, Emily. Peraco was my first home. I can't leave it like this. I could never live with myself, and you could never live with me, if I didn't go."

"Yes I can!" Her voice shook and fear was in her eyes. "I knew it, I knew it. Alex, don't go!"

"One last noble act before I officially retire as a prince." He smiled and kissed her a third time. "I have to. I love you, and you better be at the airport waiting."

"Alex!" Tears streamed down her face. "You never said you loved me."

He looked heavenward in exasperation. "Yes I have."

"No you haven't!"

He laughed, positive she was wrong, then promised, "I'll make up for it. For the rest of my life."

"Alex," Stanni said softly.

He kissed her a fourth time and whispered in her ear, "I love you, I love you, I love you. It's a half mile more to my aunt, an easy ten-minute walk. You'll be safe, Emily. I need you to do this for me, and I trust you with everything."

He let her go and ran back down the hill with Stanni.

Emily stood in front of the black and gold wrought-iron gates, staring in numb blankness at the big *L* embossed on the door shields.

She couldn't believe she was alone. Alex had gone with Stanni, and she had just stood there in shock and let him go. By the time she had come to her senses, she'd realized there was nothing she could do but finish what he'd entrusted to her hands. She clutched the velvet bag against her chest, the burden heavy, almost too heavy in its meaning.

At the end of the driveway was a white marble open-air mansion, which looked suspiciously like a temple. A tall older woman in a housedress was cutting flowers from the garden out in front.

Emily was about to call to the woman when several men, materializing from nowhere and yelling at her in Greek, ran toward her. She stepped back a pace, fear tightening her stomach. She had a feeling her "bones in the basket" repertoire would get her into real trouble now.

"Please, may I see Julia Kiros?" she asked when the men reached the gate, then remembered her manners. "Her Royal Highness, I mean. Her nephew Alex . . . and Stanni sent me."

The men stared at her as if dumbstruck.

The older woman walked toward them, clearly having overheard her. Large dogs rose from their hidden snoozing places and followed her.

"I'm Julia Kiros," the woman said. She was almost mannish in her build, and blue-gray hair peeped out from the large straw hat she wore. "Let her in, you louts! Can't you see she's here for me?"

"But, Your Royal Highness," one said, "you know Monsieur Lemos's orders. You shouldn't even be outside—"

"Oh, poth and bother." She waved a hand in dismissal while smiling at Emily. "Let the child in. It's Emily, isn't it?"

Emily blinked in astonishment. "Ah, yes. Yes, it is."

"Then you must come in."

Within seconds, she found herself inside the estate of one of the richest men in the world, the gate clanging shut behind her. The men glared at her, but the four dogs, huge wolfhounds, nearly knocked her over with their enthusiastic greeting.

"Down, you monsters!" Her Royal Highness shouted, flailing the animals with a pink peony. When the dogs settled, she turned to Emily, taking her arm and drawing her into a rough hug. "I've heard a lot about you from that scamp Stanni. He didn't do you justice, my dear. Trust Alex to find a gem at last."

"I have something for you," Emily said, finally finding her voice. She offered the bag to Julia, her hands shaking as she realized the importance of what she held. It had been so remote before, left in Alex's capable hands. With the kind of rotten luck she'd had so far, it was a miracle she'd made the last half mile uneventfully.

Julia took the bag and opened it. "Excellent. My nephew did well. But then I knew he would."

"He went back. With Stanni. To Peraco." Her cheeks felt wet. Emily realized it was from tears, and she swiped them away.

"Did he now?" Julia smiled broadly. "I'm not surprised. Alex has a lot of honor." She put her arm around Emily and walked her toward the house. "Don't worry. Nothing will happen to him— except that he'll be a hero." She laughed. "I'll bet he never expected that!"

"Neither did I," Emily said glumly.

"He'll be home with you before you know it. Now come in and have some tea."

Two months later Emily knew the truth. Despite what Julia had said, Alex wasn't coming.

Because he didn't want to.

Every day the pain in her heart grew worse. She had known, had always known, it would come to an end with him. But the bitter knife still twisted, leaving huge chunks of her numb until she could barely function.

She couldn't even muster any satisfaction from the fact that once the coronation jewels were revealed to be in the rightful heir's hands—as if a gift from the gods—the people of Peraco had rallied en masse and the army had literally up and quit on Florian. He was the one in exile now, and Julia was back in Peraco. She'd been there for almost two weeks.

Emily had actually seen Alex on TV, so she knew he was all right. But he hadn't called. Hadn't written. Hadn't anything. She had vowed that when he let go, she would accept it.

As she gazed at the expectant faces of her students, an all too familiar lump of unshed tears clogged her throat. Accepting it was impossible. She never would.

"Tell us the story again, Miss Cooper," Danny Pulaski called, disrupting her thoughts.

"Yes! Tell us! Pleasssssse!" her class added in a jumble of voices.

Emily realized she'd been off in "la-la land," as she often told her daydreaming students. At least their la-las had to be more pleasant. She adopted her stern teacher's demeanor. "You are supposed to be practicing writing your lower-case k. You couldn't have finished the page yet."

Papers waved frantically in the air. "We did. Honest. Pleassseee!"

She looked at the eager children and melted.

"You guys! Okay, since we've done all our handwriting . . ."

She made a face. Everyone made one back at her.

". . . I'll tell the story *again*." She sighed. They never tired of it. She had told an adult version in the Teachers' Room. Alex had been right; she hadn't been able not to tell. But her colleagues had been much more skeptical.

She pulled her desk chair over to the storytelling spot on the rug in the front of the room. The children scrambled out of their seats and sat Indian-style on the rug in front of her.

She began, "Once there was a lady named Emily who washed cats, taught twenty *very well behaved* kindergartners, and helped mommy horses bring their babies into the world—"

"Was there a lot of blood?" Richard Harper asked, right on cue. His progressive parents had videotaped the birth of his little brother, and Richard had seen it nine times.

Emily shook her head. "Hardly any."

"Oh." His face fell. She had a feeling he asked each time in hopes of tripping her up.

"She also met a prince," Emily said, going back to the story. "He was an odd prince, not like the others—"

"I think I should resent that," said a deep male voice from the doorway.

Emily glanced up and her heart seemed to burst with happiness. Alex stood in the doorway, alive and well. And smiling at her.

"Alex," she whispered. For a moment the room hazed over a dull gray, then it came back sharp and bright and vivid. And filled with him.

She jumped from her chair and ran toward him,

leaping over her kids, who screamed and giggled in delight. He met her halfway and then she was in his arms, his lips on hers firmly, reassuringly, and she forgot everything.

"Omigod, omigod, Alex," she chanted over and over, kissing him frantically. "I thought you weren't coming back. I thought you didn't want me."

"I thought you didn't want me. You weren't at the airport."

"I didn't know, I didn't know."

"Didn't they call you?"

"No." She hugged him tighter, not caring about delinquent messengers.

"Is that the prince?" she heard a boy ask.

"He doesn't look like a prince," a girl said.

"Yeah. Where's his crown?"

"Maybe his blood is blue. Do you think we could cut him and find out?"

Emily started laughing. She turned around. "Not a chance, Richard. And, yes, this is the prince. And, no, he doesn't wear a crown—"

"Miss Cooper won't let me," Alex said. He swept her up in his arms.

Emily yelped and grabbed his shoulders.

He looked right into her eyes. "But I think I'll make her Princess Emily anyway."

"Yahhhh!" the kids cheered, and gathered around them.

"Are you sure?" she asked over the shouting.

"Very." He smiled and kissed her softly, gently, his mouth so sweet, she thought she'd die from it.

She hugged him. "I've got to change the end of my story."

"I've got a better ending."

And he did.

Epilogue

"I feel like an imposter," Emily said.

Alex glanced up and down his wife's body with all the leisurely pleasure of a new husband. She was dressed in a black strapless gown. She called the material "crepe-do-cling," and she was right. The bodice clung to the generous curves of her breasts, dipping between them to end just at her breastbone. It was trimmed in gold, as was the hem. The gown molded tightly to her body. A little too tightly to suit his possessiveness, but he had to admit she looked stunning. Every bit a princess at Peraco's coronation ball.

The huge ballroom was filled with princesses and princes and many other dignitaries. The last count had it at over five hundred guests. None were as beautiful as Emily, though. And the designer had promised him the bodice would not fall. Emily claimed he'd used Super Glue.

"You're perfect," he declared. He pulled her to him and spun her around the marbled floor to the strains of a waltz.

"Princess Emily just doesn't sound right," she said.

"It's no worse than my mother, Princess Phyllis. The truth is, you're really a computer programmer's wife, Emily. Think you can live with it?"

"Absolutely. I love you, not the title."

"You better," he whispered in her ear.

The waltz ended, and they sought out Stanni and Tuno, whom Julia had "unretired" as major-domo. Stanni was his usual calm, cool self, while the older man was looking flushed and pleased.

"We have done well, have we not?" Tuno asked, all dressed up in his palace uniform.

"We have." Alex rocked on his heels and flipped back the tails of his ultra-formal tuxedo. He hated to admit Tuno had been right about him and his familial devotion, but he had.

"How's Blanche?" Emily asked. "And the kittens?"

"Trouble. They've shredded every stick of furniture." He shook a finger at them. "When I think of that night, all of you leaving and those damned idiots of your uncle's going across the street to the wrong house, and I was stuck delivering seven kittens. I almost wish I'd been arrested rather than left to deal with those little . . ." He paused, then brightened. ". . . *Bart Simpsons!*"

"Have you been giving him more lessons?" Alex asked his wife.

Emily just grinned.

Tuno snagged a passing man, who was dressed similarly to him. The man was small and his gaze darted nervously around the room. "Miss Emily," Tuno said, "here is someone you need to meet. This is Pieter, the man who got the crown jewels out of the palace. Pieter, Her Highness, Princess Emily."

"Oh!" Emily exclaimed, then took the man's hand and smiled warmly at him. "You were incredibly brave, Pieter, and you saved your country."

He smiled shyly. "Thank you, Your Highness. I was . . . honored to do what I had to do."

"You did well," Alex told him, not fussing because it seemed inappropriate. He'd leave the fussing to Emily.

"Attention!" The Crown Princess Julia's voice boomed out over the crowd. Everyone turned toward the musicians' stage, where Julia stood, resplendent in a white gown, the crown atop her gray hair. "We are pleased to be home and pleased to have the country back with the people. All were brave and we commend each of you for your diligence in upholding the constitution of Peraco. We are grateful to those of the royal family who worked hard and risked their lives for us . . ."

Emily touched the Order of the Star medallion hanging from a sash over Alex's chest. He covered her hand with his. His aunt had bestowed the highest medal of honor on him for his service in bringing out the crown jewels and coming back to organize a rebellion. He'd never once doubted that Emily had been with him throughout that time, even though half a world had separated them. He was proud to have come to her afterward without a shadow of regret.

". . . We have given many honors and have many honors yet to give," Julia continued, then smiled. "However, at this time, we are pleased to bestow on the newest member of the family, Emily, Princess of Kiros, her own title of Countess in recognition of her outstanding service to the Crown. Emily, child, come here."

Emily gaped as Julia beckoned her forward. Alex nudged her. "You never keep a Crown Princess waiting."

"Right."

Alex escorted his wife to the podium and watched with pride as Julia honored Emily with her own title. By elevating her to nobility, Julia was giving royal approval of the marriage. When it was over, Alex led Emily away and winked at her. The "Peracanization" of Emily was now complete. "Think you'll still like being married to a lowly computer programmer now that you're a countess?"

She leaned against him and kissed him shyly. "Always. I love you."

He gazed raptly at her as a collage of Emilys ran through his mind. Emily laughing. Emily defiant. Emily straight-faced and "innocent." Emily furious. Emily soft and loving. There were more, and they were all the infinite facets of his Emily.

"I love you," he whispered, and kissed her temple.

"And now we would like also to honor our personal bodyguards," Julia said, interrupting their quiet moment.

The four wolfhounds came bounding in from the terrace, woofing and scrambling across the marbled floor. They leaped on guests and generally attempted to scrape the clothes from their bodies.

"My babies," Julia cooed, calling them to her. "Mommy has some nice bones for you."

Cameras went off in a strobe light of flashes, capturing the royal moment for posterity . . .

and the front pages of newspapers around the world.

Alex looked at Emily in horror.

"You're plain vanilla," she told him firmly.

"You're sure?"

"Forever." She kissed his cheek. "I wouldn't have it any other way."

THE EDITOR'S CORNER

◆ **Late-Breaking News** ◆

The Delaney dynasty continues!
THE DELANEY CHRISTMAS CAROL
by Kay Hooper, Iris Johansen, and Fayrene Preston.
Three NEW stories of Delaney Christmases
past, present, and future.

On sale in paperback from Bantam FANFARE
in November.

◆

There's a kind of hero we all love, the kind who usually wears irresistible tight jeans and holds a less-than-glamorous job. The world doesn't always sing his praises, but the world couldn't do without him—and next month LOVESWEPT salutes him with MEN AT WORK. In six fabulous new romances that feature only these men on the covers, you'll meet six heroes who are unique in many ways, yet are all hardworking, hard-driving, and oh, so easy to love!

First, let Billie Green sweep you away to Ireland, where you'll meet a hunk of a sheep farmer, Keith Donegal. He's the **MAN FROM THE MIST,** LOVESWEPT #564, and Jenna Howard wonders if his irresistible heat is just a spell woven by the land of leprechauns. But with dazzling kisses and thrilling caresses, Keith sets out to prove that the fire between them is the real thing. The magic of Billie's writing shines through in this enchanting tale of love and desire.

In **BUILT TO LAST** by Lori Copeland, LOVESWEPT #565, the hero, Bear Malone, is exactly what you would expect from his name—big, eye-catching, completely fascinating, and with a heart to match his size. A carpenter, he renovates houses for poor families, and he admires the feisty beauty Christine Brighton for volunteering for the job. Now, if he can only convince her that they should make a home and a family of their own . . . Lori makes a delightful and sensual adventure out of building a house.

You'll get plenty of **MISCHIEF AND MAGIC** in Patt Bucheister's new LOVESWEPT, #566. Construction worker Phoenix Sierra knows all about mischief from his friends' practical jokes, and when he lands in an emergency room because of one, he finds magic in Deborah Justin. The copper-haired doctor is enticing, but before she will love Phoenix, he must reveal the vulnerable man hiding behind his playboy facade. You'll keep turning the pages as Patt skillfully weaves this tale of humor and passion.

Kimberli Wagner returns to LOVESWEPT with **A COWBOY'S TOUCH,** LOVESWEPT #567, and as before, she is sure to enchant you with her provocative writing and ability to create sizzling tension. In this story, Jackie Stone ends up working as the cook on her ex-husband's ranch because she desperately needs the money. But Gray Burton has learned from his mistakes, and he'll use a cowboy's touch to persuade Jackie to return to his loving arms. Welcome back, Kim!

There can't be a more perfect—or sexy—title for a book in which the hero is an electric lineman than **DANGEROUS IN THE DARK** by Terry Lawrence, LOVESWEPT #568. Zach Young is a lineman for the county, the one to call when the lights go out. When he gets caught in an electric storm, he finds shelter in Candy Wharton's isolated farmhouse. He makes Candy feel safe in the dark; the danger is in allowing him into her heart. All the stirring emotions that you've come to expect from Terry are in this fabulous story.

Olivia Rupprecht gives us a memorable gift of love with **SAINTS AND SINNERS,** LOVESWEPT #569. Matthew

Peters might be a minister, but he's no saint—and he's determined to get to know gorgeous Delilah Sampson, who's just moved in across the street from his Iowa church. He's as mortal as the next man, and he can't ignore a woman who's obviously in trouble . . . or deny himself a taste of fierce passion. Once again, Olivia delivers an enthralling, powerful romance.

On sale this month from FANFARE are four breathtaking novels. **A WHOLE NEW LIGHT** proves why Sandra Brown is a *New York Times* bestselling author. In this story, widow Cyn McCall wants to shake up her humdrum life, but when Worth Lansing asks her to spend a weekend with him in Acapulco, she's more than a little surprised—and tempted. Worth had always been her friend, her late husband's business partner. What will happen when she sees him in a whole new light?

Award-winning author Rosanne Bittner sets **THUNDER ON THE PLAINS** in one of America's greatest eras—the joining of the East and West by the first transcontinental railroad. Sunny Landers is the privileged daughter of a powerful railroad magnate. Colt Travis is the half-Indian scout who opens her eyes to the beauty and danger of the West . . . and opens her heart to love.

INTIMATE STRANGERS is a gripping and romantic time-travel novel by Alexandra Thorne. On vacation in Santa Fe, novelist Jane Howard slips into a flame-colored dress and finds herself transported to 1929, in another woman's life, in her home . . . and with her husband.

Critically acclaimed author Patricia Potter creates a thrilling historical romance with **LIGHTNING**. During the Civil War, nobody was a better blockade runner for the South than Englishman Adrian Cabot, but Lauren Bradly swore to stop him. Together they would be swept into passion's treacherous sea, tasting deeply of ecstasy and the danger of war.

Also on sale this month, in the hardcover edition from Doubleday, is **SINFUL** by Susan Johnson. Sweeping from the majestic manors of England to the forbidden salons of a Tunisian harem, this is a tale of desperate deception and sensual pleasures between a daring woman and a passionate nobleman.

Happy reading!

With best wishes,

Nita Taublib
Associate Publisher
LOVESWEPT and FANFARE

The Delaney Dynasty lives on in

The Delaney Christmas Carol

by Kay Hooper, Iris Johansen, & Fayrene Preston

Three of romantic fiction's best-loved authors present the changing face of Christmas spirit—past, present, and future—as they tell the story of three generations of Delaneys in love.

CHRISTMAS PAST by Iris Johansen

From the moment he first laid eyes on her, Kevin Delaney felt a curious attraction to the ragclad Gypsy beauty rummaging through the attic of his ranch at Killara. He didn't believe for a moment her talk of magic mirrors and second-sight, but something about Zara St. Cloud stirred his blood. Now, as Christmas draws near, a touch leads to a kiss and a gift of burning passion.

CHRISTMAS PRESENT by Fayrene Preston

Bria Delaney had been looking for Christmas ornaments in her mother's attic, when she saw him in the mirror for the first time—a stunningly handsome man with sky-blue eyes and red-gold hair. She had almost convinced herself he was only a dream when Kells Braxton arrived at Killara and led them both to a holiday wonderland of sensuous pleasure.

CHRISTMAS FUTURE by Kay Hooper

As the last of the Delaney men, Brett returned to Killara this Christmastime only to find it in the capable hands of his father's young and beautiful widow. Yet the closer he got to Cassie, the more Brett realized that the embers of their old love still burned and that all it would take was a look, a kiss, a caress, to turn their dormant passion into an inferno.

The best in Women's Fiction from Bantam FANFARE.
On sale in November 1992   AN 428 8/92

FANFARE

On Sale in July

A WHOLE NEW LIGHT

☐ 29783-X $5.99/6.99 in Canada
by Sandra Brown

<u>New York Times</u> bestselling author

Under the romantic skies of Acapulco, Cyn McCall and Worth Lansing succumb to blazing passion in one reckless moment, and must face the fears and doubts that threaten to shatter their new and fragile bond.

THUNDER ON THE PLAINS

☐ 29015-0 $5.99/6.99 in Canada
by Rosanne Bittner

"Emotional intensity and broad strokes of color...a strong historical saga and a powerful romance. Ms. Bittner [is] at the top of her form."
-- <u>Romantic Times</u>

INTIMATE STRANGERS

☐ 29519-5 $4.99/5.99 in Canada
by Alexandra Thorne

"Talented author Alexandra Thorne has written a complex and emotionall intense saga of reincarnation and time travel, where it just might be possible to correct the errors of time." -- <u>Romantic Times</u>

LIGHTNING

☐ 29070-3 $4.99/5.99 in Canada
by Patricia Potter

Their meeting was fated. Lauren Bradley was sent by Washington to sabotage Adrian Cabot's Confederate ship...he was sent by destiny to steal her heart. Together they are swept into passion's treacherous sea

☐ Please send me the books I have checked above. I am enclosing $ _____ (add $2.50 to cov postage and handling). Send check or money order, no cash or C. O. D.'s please.

Mr./ Ms._____

Address_____

City/ State/ Zip_____

Send order to: Bantam Books, Dept. FN 59, 2451 S. Wolf Rd., Des Plaines, IL 60018

Allow four to six weeks for delivery.

Prices and availability subject to change without notice.

THE SYMBOL OF GREAT WOMEN'S
FICTION FROM BANTAM

Ask for these books at your local bookstore or use this page to order. FN 59 8/92

FANFARE

On Sale in August

DAWN ON A JADE SEA
☐ 29837-2 $5.50/6.50 in Canada
by Jessica Bryan
bestselling author of ACROSS A WINE-DARK SEA

She was a shimmering beauty from a kingdom of legend. A vision had brought Rhea to the glorious city of Ch'ang-an, compelling her to seek a green-eyed, auburn-haired foreign warrior called Zhao, the Red Tiger. Amid the jasmine of the Imperial Garden, passion will be born, hot as fire, strong as steel, eternal as the ocean tides.

BLAZE
☐ 29957-3 $5.50/6.50 in Canada
by Susan Johnson
bestselling author of FORBIDDEN and SINFUL

To Blaze Braddock, beautiful, pampered daughter of a millionaire, the American gold rush was a chance to flee the stifling codes of Boston society. But when Jon Hazard Black, a proud young Absarokee chief, challenged her father's land claim, Blaze was swept up in a storm of passions she had never before even imagined.

LAST BRIDGE HOME
☐ 29871-2 $4.50/5.50 in Canada
by Iris Johansen
bestselling author of THE GOLDEN BARBARIAN

Jon Sandell is a man with many secrets and one remarkable power, the ability to read a woman's mind, to touch her soul, to know her every waking desire. His vital mission is to rescue a woman unaware of the danger she is in. But who will protect her from him?

FANFARE

The Very Best in Historical Women's Fiction

Rosanne Bittner

_____	28599-8 EMBERS OF THE HEART	$4.50/5.50 in Canada
_____	28319-7 MONTANA WOMAN	$4.99/5.99
_____	29033-9 IN THE SHADOW OF THE MOUNTAINS	$5.50/6.99
_____	29014-2 SONG OF THE WOLF	$4.99/5.99
_____	29015-0 THUNDER ON THE PLAINS	$5.99/6.99

Kay Hooper

_____	29256-0 THE MATCHMAKER	$4.50/5.50

Iris Johansen

_____	28855-5 THE WIND DANCER	$4.95/5.95
_____	29032-0 STORM WINDS	$4.99/5.99
_____	29244-7 REAP THE WIND	$4.99/5.99
_____	29604-3 THE GOLDEN BARBARIAN	$4.99/5.99

Teresa Medeiros

_____	29047-5 HEATHER AND VELVET	$4.99/5.99

Patricia Potter

_____	29070-3 LIGHTNING	$4.99/5.99
_____	29071-1 LAWLESS	$4.99/5.99
_____	29069-X RAINBOW	$4.99/5.99

Fayrene Preston

_____	29332-X THE SWANSEA DESTINY	$4.50/5.50

Amanda Quick

_____	29325-7 RENDEZVOUS	$4.99/5.99
_____	28354-5 SEDUCTION	$4.99/5.99
_____	28932-2 SCANDAL	$4.95/5.95
_____	28594-7 SURRENDER	$4.50/5.50

Deborah Smith

_____	28759-1 THE BELOVED WOMAN	$4.50/5.50

Ask for these titles at your bookstore or use this page to order.

Please send me the books I have checked above. I am enclosing $ _____ (add $2.50 to cover postage and handling). Send check or money order, no cash or C. O. D.'s please.

Mr./ Ms. _____

Address _____

City/ State/ Zip _____

Send order to: Bantam Books, Dept. FN 17, 2451 S. Wolf Road, Des Plaines, IL 60018

Please allow four to six weeks for delivery.

Prices and availability subject to change without notice.

FN 17 - 8/92